Nostradamus
Vagabond Prophet

A Novel of His Life and Time

Allene Symons

Forked Road Press

for Wanda, always

Nostradamus
Vagabond Prophet

Prologue

Paris, 1559

I Alain Saint-Germain am not given to prophetic visions. Only once in a childhood dream did I catch a single future glimpse. In that dream I saw the garden of Michel de Nostredame mobbed by an angry crowd that held aloft the charred effigy of a man. A terrifying vision, but one diminished by daylight and forgotten until a June day many decades later.

I recall the dream and the day; the smell of burning rags and timbers, the voices of men crying out for revenge. Odd, how memory is snared by a scent or a sound such as the crumbling embers that warm me on this last day of the old year. Journals, yellowed and torn, lie on the table before me and beside them, a few rare letters from my friend Michel. Together they will goad me to complete this account, a task I have long intended to accomplish.

That June day in 1559 began ill-omened. Why did I not suspect a tragic turn of event? Above the towers of Les Tournelles, heavy storm clouds marred the early sky in prelude to a wedding celebration that should have been blessed by sunlight, not shrouded in gray.

I recall that the weather made us all uneasy.

Catherine, the Queen Consort, reclined within her lavish suite surrounded by bed drapes of vermilion satin. I had carried a message to her from the King and was told to wait, so I listened from across the room while the Florentine chef confirmed elaborate plans for serving peacock and other delicacies to a thousand guests. Many had traveled far to celebrate the ceremony bonding two countries by the nuptial mass, for Princess Elizabeth was to be joined with Phillip, King of Spain, and King Henri's sister, Marguerite, to Phillip's ally, the Duke of Savoy.

I watched as the dressmaker arrived with her assistants to display the narrow-thread lace that had been added to bridal gowns and trains the night before. The Queen nodded approval but showed no sign of pleasure over the remarkable lacework, usually one of her passions.

Since one of the slashes on my shoe was poorly cut and bit into my foot, I shifted my weight. From where I stood, I could see the Queen's troubled face and knew more than dark clouds concerned her. I had delivered Michel's book called *The Prophecies* to her myself. She was aware of the cryptic four-line poems, and in particular the quatrain that read:

> *The Young Lion will overcome the Old*
> *By a single duel in a martial field*
> *His eye will be rent in a Golden Cage*
> *Two wounds from one, the cruel death is sealed*

You will need no interpretation now that fact stands in place of prophecy, yet remember on that morning Michel's words remained unfulfilled. In those days, one did not take such predictions lightly.

Many of his forecasts too often had proven true, and though each quatrain was obscure, this one was clearer than most; thus Catherine interpreted King Henri to be the Old Lion, but she puzzled over the place and time of death in a martial field, for these were times of peace.

After the long wait, and because my foot was asleep, I cleared my throat to see if the Queen had forgotten me. Startled, she looked up and said, "Go, you are no longer needed." As I prepared to take my leave and return to other court duties, I saw her replace the message in a drawer in her bedside cabinet and remove a pouch containing a moonstone. She rubbed the milky agate between thumb and forefinger, for someone once told her the stone would ward off sadness.

By late morning as the appointed hour of the tournament drew near, the canopy of clouds parted and ladies no longer worried for their frocks. The jousting tourney on the Rue Saint-Antoine was the only nuptial event held outside the compound walls. It was an exercise in honor favored by the King and welcomed by guests who otherwise would spend three days feasting to the point of bilious discomfort.

For their viewing pleasure, three-tiered wooden scaffolds had been built around the perimeter of the field. Seats were hung with bright flags or festooned with colored bunting. When the sun reached its apogee, the streets lay nearly deserted but the scaffold seats brimmed with spectators. Upon rooftops, from windows and over the tops of turrets for a great distance around the field, you could see clusters of men and women waiting to view the traditional mock battle.

As the wedding ceremony created alliances and glorified the two brides, the tournament was staged to enhance King Henri's magnificence. For the monarch, facing his forty-first year, the tourney alone was reason to spend several thousand ducats. But his money's worth was not to be gained sitting in the royal stand and reviewing captains who had already won glory on the battlefield.

With aid from his grooms, Henri mounted his steed, a proud white creature familiar with the weight of a man and full armor, but today burdened also with a chestpiece fashioned of silver on scalloped, tasseled brocade. Beneath the tassels the stallion reared and stamped its hooves, raising columns of dust around its snowy fetlocks.

Henri jabbed his jeweled shoe into the horse's flank and sent it trotting heavily toward the point of combat. Two pairs of trumpeters blew six shrill notes into the air, stilling conversation in the stands. All eyes followed the King as he passed the tier where his mistress, the Lady Diane, sat serenely in a black and white gown that belied two decades of widow's mourning. The King paused below and lowered his helmet in her direction and then turned the horse abruptly and rode to a halt beneath the royal stand.

The Queen leaned forward in her seat and appeared as if to speak, but instead threw her husband a rose that he plucked from the air and thrust beneath a flap of leather on his saddle.

Applause rose from the throng, expressing approval of Henri's perfect form in the spirit of the day's match, for it promised no winner save the King. To unseat him would be unthinkable.

The tourney began, and in three artful sweeps of the wooden wall, the Duc de Guise lost to Henri. The Duke's lance touched lightly upon the royal armor, then veered off and jammed into the wall with a crack we could hear even over hoof beats. It was a grand exhibition to see the monarch in combat, parrying his weapon with power and elegance, and I imagined that few spectators appreciated the challenge to his opponents, for their mastery of the lance was exceptional—that of men who could succumb yet leave an impression of hard-gained royal victory.

Murmuring began in the stands again between the first and second tilts. Servants threaded through the rows with fans to cool the ladies, for now the June heat was bearing down through a patchy, clouded sky. Attendants rushed onto the field to clear away remnants of the duke's broken lance and smooth out potholes with iron rakes.

The second round began with the Duke of Savoy riding against the King. The duke was an excellent rider who maneuvered his own defeat and drove his roan as if life depended on the contest's outcome, delving his spurs into the roan's flank and sending the beast into great, lumbering strides. A fine act! (I do not mean to slight the King's effort. A joust is no mean feat, and he was no doubt as tired as was his mount with its foam-stippled coat.)

As the King's third lance broke on the Duke's arm guard, the crowd cheered thunderously, thinking this last pass marked the end of the exhibition, but in the din of applause Henri stood up in his stirrups, waved his hand high in a sign of endurance and sent his groom across the field to speak with an officer named Montgomery, Captain of the King's Scots Guard.

I looked to the stand where Mary, the beautiful Queen of Scots and daughter of King James, sat beside the Dauphin, Henri's son. The girl smiled encouragingly toward her countryman Montgomery, though the prince at her side frowned with concern. Montgomery himself seemed surprised that the King would engage in yet another contest. Three rounds would exhaust a far younger rider. But no one was empowered to curb his excess, and in short order a fresh horse was led alongside. Henri waved it away then spurred his mount across the tourney field into position at the end of the wooden barrier that separated combatants during the pass and prevented a collision between oncoming horses.

Montgomery rode to the opposite end and angled his lance for the first encounter. The King urged his horse into a heavy gallop along the wall, aiming his weapon for advantage, his weight forward as was the King's usual style before a parry. The plumes adorning his silver helmet sagged from accumulated dust.

As the King and his captain closed in on the testing point, a sun-shaft broke through the clouds and struck the King's helmet like molten gold. I heard Montgomery's lance break against the King's armor and watched in horror as the tip of the lance splintered into deadly prongs and knifed sharply through the King's visor.

Henri dropped the reins, slumped forward onto the horse's neck, and desperately clasped the beast with one arm until from habit the horse slowed near the end of the course, blood streaming down its neck.

The crowd stood, the field filled with men, and someone stopped the horse in time to catch its falling rider. They tore off the silver helmet, and I could see no more behind the throng until a litter arrived and they carried the King away.

TEN NIGHTS LATER, the populace stood in vigil outside the walls of Les Tournelles. Some held out hope for the King's life, but mostly old women who knelt before the palace gates and wailed prayers, expecting a miracle. Before sunrise, news of the monarch's death spread through the throng. I keened my ears to the din below and from the milling crowd I heard a vengeful cry: "Accursed be he who prophesied the King's dying so evilly and so well!"

With fear and a certain fascination I considered slipping into the crowd like Nostradamus's curious double, but I knew what I would see, and that I would only return stinking of smoke but be no wiser for watching ignorant cabans banking their pyres.

Instead, I raged inwardly at the hypocrisy of people who clamored in the marketplace for copies of *The Prophecies,* those who paid coins for forecasts yet cared only for the fantastical, and when the words were fulfilled, cursed Nostradamus for his verity. They condemned him as a dealer in dark magic, yet I had long known him as a man of faith and high aspiration, a devoted husband and enduring friend.

In an earlier, youthful time of our lives when we talked lightly of our futures, I had spoken of writing poetry in the hope that one day my name would be known across this land—yet Michel was the one who had attained fame through his quatrains. No, he had embraced infamy. Yet so distorted was my countrymen's conception of him on that June night that I vowed, as I stood on the balcony with smoke stinging my eyes, to someday tell the true and entire story of my friendship with Michel de Nostredame.

Finally I am disposed to do it. I call upon memory and imagination to aid me when journals and letters provide insufficient record, but I will be forgiven this liberty by anyone who has read Michel's work, for they already know a poet's truth is not the same as everyman's.

The Pathways to Prophecy

IN OUR NATAL VILLAGE of Saint-Rémy, when my tutor had gone and my daily tasks were done, I would run along the cobbled streets toward Michel's home with sandals striking against unyielding stones. Recalling those years conjures forth a courtyard garden where boxwood hedges portioned off the vegetable garden and vines of morning glory sprawled along ginger-colored walls, where olive trees and flowering plum offered shade and new grass thrust up bright spires from the moist, dark sod.

Behind the garden stood a solidly built storage room with walls thicker than those of the living quarters. Michel's father, Jaume de Nostredame, had constructed it with raised slat floors to protect the grain from dampness, and it had openings beneath the eaves, set at an angle, to allow ventilation yet prevent rain from spoiling his stores of barley, wheat and millet. It was an unusual granary, and I have seen none like it since; thus was the family of Michel de Nostredame inclined to devise clever solutions.

Michel was one of five brothers, but only he showed an early gift for scholarship and therefore was exempt from toiling in his father's trade. The family expected their eldest son to study medicine, and to this end he was instructed by his grandfather, Jean de Saint-Rémy, who once served as physician to a noble family.

Our families were bonded by membership in the rising class of merchants among whom gold replaced the fraternity of noble blood. Yet within the brotherhood of merchants there were distinctions.

In those days, Michel's family was not as wealthy as mine, but Jaume de Nostredame provided his wife and children with a comfortable living and they suffered no lack. They owned their dwelling and the adjacent land housing the granary, and Michel's father did a steady trade. Michel's mother was a frail woman with serene gray eyes like those of her eldest son.

Due in part to her health and his devotion to her, Jaume rarely ventured forth on buying trips and instead relied on his assistants to procure the goods that he sold throughout Provence. His concern for Michel's mother and for his sons gave Jaume a stern countenance. He was nonetheless a kind and generous man but like my own father, stubborn and practical-minded.

Their home was not large, but solid and well crafted. In the warming room—the kitchen—table and chairs glowed from careful polishing. Gleaming brass utensils and bundles of onions and herbs hung from beams spanning the whitewashed walls, and one could count on meals both ample and satisfying.

Our homes were similar in appointment, though mine was larger as befit my father's income. I had an entire small room to myself, while Michel had a cozy storage space up a ladder off the kitchen.

The land of Provence, once under the sway of Imperial Rome, later became a home to troubadours who many years before my time spread their tales of heroes and fancy. But I have Michel's family to thank for my own interest in scholarship and the love of words that set me on my course. My family set less store by learning, and as I grew older I had to convince them that an educated son could burnish the family's reputation.

Michel's family needed no convincing of the importance of education, and indeed my friend was naturally gifted in languages and mathematics. As a boy he studied with his learned grandfather, and I recall the day when I stumbled onto the great difference between our two families, a difference of which I had only heard my parents whisper.

❧

ONE SUNNY APRIL day in the year 1518, Michel's grandfather carried his cherished books into a corner of the garden, where he began instructing Michel in the writings of the Hebrews, the Romans and the Greeks.

Arriving unnoticed, I had decided not to disturb them. I spied a soft mossy place behind a tree and sat there, out of view, to wait for the conclusion of Michel's lesson. The sun was past the high point of noon, and I knew the old man usually closed his books when the sun reached the top of a certain olive tree in the garden.

"Grandfather," Michel asked, "is the *apeiron* of Anaximander the same as the *olam* of the Hebrews?"

The old man paused then answered cautiously: "*Olam* means boundless time, an endless time which stretches from the past to the future, but Anaximander writes of extension without end. To him, *apeiron* means boundless space."

"But if they are both without limit, then why are time and space not the same?"

"Wise men say they are, yet our words bind us with limitations." The old man's eyes wandered skyward toward a passing wisp of cloud. I wondered if he was losing his celebrated faculties, but he was pausing before drawing his grandson into a line of argument.

"Michel, do you know why I want to conduct our lesson in the garden today?"

He replied curtly, "No, for I am a better pupil in the house where I am not distracted by flies."

"Do you find no beauty in this day?"

"Springtime makes men into fools," Michel said, then regretting his disrespectful tone of voice added, "Wouldn't Plato agree that we only see shadows thrown on walls, dancing images to seduce us from truth?"

I sat beneath my tree and listened to a brooding side of my friend beyond my understanding. Michel and I were an unlikely pair. He was inclined to play solitary games or to labor over his books. Convincing him to join me in countryside explorations required constant effort, and when I finally persuaded him to come along, he carried along his ever-present notebook and inscribed observations, curious mainly about the oddities and flaws of nature.

"You misinterpret Plato's words," said the grandfather." Beauty need not lead you from truth, but in it you may glimpse the greater Form which lures you toward itself. Tomorrow you shall reread *The Symposium*, and this time know Plato's mind on the meaning of the beautiful."

I heard Michel grumbling over the assignment. I knew that though he loved his studies, he was looking forward to the next morning when he had been promised a taster's part in the preparation of the season's first quince jam. Even now, mounds of fruit sat nested inside baskets in his mother's kitchen, awaiting the homely alchemy that would transform them into Michel's favorite delicacy; indeed, my friend was easily seduced by the wonders of the palate and enjoyed experimenting with recipes, spices, herbs and flavors.

But when he began to speak out in defense of the long-awaited day, his grandfather silenced him. I peeked out to see the old man gathering smooth stones from the garden and eleven twigs, one longer than the rest.

"Think of these rocks and branches as the Tree of Life—"

I thought to myself this is nonsense. Stones and dead bark could never make a tree, not in God's nature.

"—for all materials transcend the words by which we know them. No object is what it seems to a man who forbids time and place to bind him, a man whose home is not marked on any map."

The old physician inhaled a breath and slowly said, "It is time to talk again of the Mysteries and of your ancient heritage."

This sounded like foolishness to me, even though the old man's voice was rhythmic and strangely compelling. Were these mysteries and the arrangement of garden debris the elements of some dark magic? I had heard rumors. Michel and his family attended Mass and followed the faith, or did it only seem so? I had overheard my parents saying that Michel's great-grandfather was a Jew who had converted to our faith rather than lose his land and face expulsion.

Michel and his grandfather were unaware that I listened as they spoke, yet now I stood as witness while the old man drew my friend into some strange rite.

Apparently the teacher of Greek, Latin and mathematics had another purpose up his sly old sleeve.

For a moment I was afraid, fearing my soul would shrivel for being a bystander. But why should I anticipate evil? Perhaps this was only another kind of faith, oddly appearing to an outsider. And if I thought about it, wasn't my own faith peculiar? Even I became confused when I paused to consider the mystery of an omnipotent God who could somehow reside in the temporal body of a man, His Son.

"Mi-ka-el," the old man intoned, "your namesake was leader of the Tribe of Issachar, the accursed ones who bought comfort and peace by wearing the yoke of captors rather than choosing the lean freedom of their faith. Do not forget this lesson in weakness. Listen for a sign from your heart."

At that moment, from my mossy spot under the tree, I sneezed. Crimson-faced, I leaped from behind the olive tree and tried to appear as though I had just arrived through the garden gate. Startled, Michel sprang from the ground as the old man destroyed his emblem with the quick sweep of a gnarled hand.

"Draper's boy, why do you hide?" asked the old one, seeing through my ploy.

"I did not wish to disturb the lesson," I replied and then sputtered, "I also have read *The Symposium*."

At that point Michel's father and youngest brother

walked into the garden. "Is my son learning his Latin and Greek?" asked Jaume de Nostredame. "I expect him to be ahead of his schoolmates. We have set aside money for his medical education at Montpellier, and I pray that our investment will not be wasted."

"He makes progress with the classics," said the older man. "Even at this tender age his questions give me pause."

I saw a frown of doubt cross the father's brow, as though the old man's remark did not reassure him but caused further concern. I had often seen a faraway look on the face of Michel's grandfather, yet on his father's face one saw only a shrewd immediacy, as though in the modeling of their characteristics God had skipped a generation by passing the distant gaze directly from grandsire to grandson.

"I trust you are not wasting your time on fables or spurious texts," said Michel's father, "for the boy already has an overdeveloped imagination and I will not allow him to waste his true gifts."

The old man smiled. "Rest assured, I will impart to him only those lessons intended to further his true gifts. But for now, I notice that the sun has reached the top of the olive tree and it is time for my afternoon nap. These old eyes are sharpest in early light, and the draper's boy waits for Michel and Jean to join him in some afternoon adventure."

The father muttered, "No doubt join him in some folly."

At last we set out, the three of us, running across rain-puddled paths. His little brother Jean and I followed at Michel's heels in an unspoken hierarchy of leadership, with Jean and I chattering and shoving and often oblivious of our direction, while Michel walked with purpose, quietly observant and sure of his way.

He was not tall but sinewy and compact, with tawny skin, gray eyes, and a manner that could seem sullen and restless. He was strong and self-assured, even haughty at times, and more than once I bore the brunt of his withering disdain. But on that day the recriminations were aimed at the little brother whose eyes darted and glanced about, delighted by the teeming woods. Michel was intolerant of the boy's lighthearted spirit; unfairly he regarded young Jean as a simpleton enchanted by the colorful tokens of spring.

We walked through patches of blossoming broom and huddled groups of cypress. I was abreast of Michel until suddenly we became aware that one pair of footsteps was missing, which could only mean that Jean had dropped even farther behind than his usual dawdling third place.

Both of us stopped and turned to see the boy crouched over a large rock, watching something move across the sunwashed surface. Michel called out with an older brother's severity as he ran toward Jean, who with a mischievous grin raised a muddy-booted foot and smashed it down, full force, onto the unsuspecting creature.

"Idiot!" Michel raised his hand for a strike, sending Jean racing into the bushes. Michel peered at the limp green snake, its head crushed but the rest of the reptile's body unmarred. Michel retrieved it by the tail, dangling the serpent from his fingers like a green and silver cord. As his anger turned to interest, Jean and I cautiously approached to take a closer look while Michel took out a notebook and began to enter his observations.

"How flat it is," said Jean. "Why was it round like a pipe before I killed it? Was it full of air?"

"These made its shape," Michel said, grasping the uper arm of his brother, who squealed in pain.

Michel chuckled. "I was pointing out your muscle. Grandfather said in his day the Church forbade students to open cadavers for the study of muscles and organs."

I said, "You will make a fine physician someday."

"If my father has his way I will swab wounds and treat sores, but if I have my way then my profession will not be about physicking."

He threw the lifeless snake toward a nearby stand of cypress, casting it high into the air. We waited for the sound of impact but heard only the soft drone of insects. Jean and I glanced at each other and, united by curiosity, headed into the clearing to solve this mystery. Soon I found the snake draped across a jagged bough; it had never reached the ground, its projected destination.

Michel lapsed into a strangely melancholy state and continued to sit on the rock not far from where Jean had crushed the snake. A brook flowed nearby and I proposed a skipping-stone contest, but entreaty would not move Michel from his spot. The younger boy and I set off alone, promising to meet Michel later in the clearing.

When we returned he asked, "How long have I been waiting here? I have had the strangest reverie. I thought I was watching the clouds for only a short while, yet I see that it has grown late."

He was silent as we returned to the village along a gently sloping route. At a curve in the road Michel stopped and stood still as a column.

I followed his gaze toward the ground where rivulets of rain had etched delicate patterns in the soil. To me this was a pretty design and nothing more, but Michel had seen something that stopped him. I had seen him stare this way before though I had never asked why.

"We should go now," I said.

He closed his eyes; I saw his lids quiver and, thinking he might be ill, took his arm. "Leave me alone," he whispered, and opened his eyes. Whatever they saw, it must have been beautiful and terrible at the same time, for I will never forget that look on his face. Then I noticed that Jean, who liked to disturb nests and burrows, was ready for mischief so I bribed him away by offering to play a game of toss before dark.

While the sun crept below the garden wall, we threw a stuffed-leather ball back and forth. Soon I had to grope around in the shadows, pricking my fingers on rose thorns. I finally announced the last toss of our game, but before I could do so the gate swung open and Michel reappeared. He drew near, clasped my wrist in his powerful grip, and a chill coursed up my back when I realized his gray eyes had the same smoldering gaze I had once seen in the eyes of a wandering madman.

A YOUNG FELLOW was walking away from the house when I arrived as usual the next day. Michel met me at the door.

"Alain, I cannot join you today nor from now on. My father has hired a new tutor." He lowered his voice. "Though my father does not know this, I will continue to study with my grandfather every afternoon. He is expecting me now."

Bewildered by this news, I walked along with Michel in the direction of his grandfather's house, and when I turned to head back he said, "I must ask you a favor—to share my deception. Father will think I am spending time with you each day."

"I understand," I lied. Then I asked when we would see each other again.

"Only on Sundays, at Mass," he replied. "Please trust in me and in our friendship."

My home seemed gloomy that afternoon. A storm was gathering, and indoors the gray light made the polished tiles of my mother's floor look dull and sad. Even the smell of baking bread did nothing to improve my spirits.

DURING THE NEXT two years, I filled the time between lessons and supper by writing in a purloined accounts journal, where I amused myself by trying to capture thoughts and impressions in verse. Some days I worked in my father's shop, sorting heavy bolts of broadcloth, silk, linen, and wool. My arms grew stronger as I heaved the bolts from floor to storage rack with energy born of a still-lingering resentment toward Michel for expecting me to support his lies. As he predicted, we only spoke briefly on Sundays, after which he would call out for all to hear, "We will see each other tomorrow," though of course we never did.

Toward the end of the second year the old man died. Three weeks later, Michel reappeared at my door. He held a book in his hand and asked hesitantly, "May I come in?"

With reserve intended to shield me from disappointment, I motioned him to enter. My father was away, traveling in search of goods to buy cheaply and sell dear, his guiding principle and one I did not wish to emulate. I offered Michel the high-backed chair usually occupied by my father. By this formality he sensed my distance.

"Is friendship so easily lost?"

"I have done the favor you asked," I replied flatly.

"Alain," he said, "my decision of two years ago was not a simple one. Now I grieve, and I come to you for solace. I grieve for the loss of my grandfather, and you are the only person who knows the nature of our secret pact. I thought the sharing of that secret showed my trust, but perhaps I assumed too much."

My sulking suddenly struck me as foolish so I grinned, then we both began to laugh.

"It is good to see your smile," he said, handing me the book. "I brought you a gift—a new edition of François Villon."

I ran my fingers over the rich leather binding of the book of poetry, its title letters tooled in gold. "I purchased it last week in Lyons," he said, his eyes bright. "I wish you had been with me to see the latest innovations of the printer's craft. Just think of the possibility of the printed word reaching out to so many."

I turned the pages, fine sheets of rag paper printed in the newest style of type.

"You were often on my mind," he said cautiously, as if unsure of my terms. "You would have found it amusing to watch me rummaging through the books like a person possessed, much to my father's dismay. He understandably questions whether I have the proper temperament for a dedicated student of medicine."

"Well, my father has little confidence in me either," I confided. "He has disdain for what he calls my 'accumulated scraps of rhyme' and says I have no business mind, which may be true, and he accuses me of confusing warp and woof, which I deny. Worse, he cannot stand my lute, so

I have to practice while he is away."

"My absence has proven of some benefit," Michel said, and I realized he was right. The account book and the lute had become my companions. Many pages contained new poems and I had mastered numerous songs. "Soon I will attend the university in Avignon," he added, "where I will board with my cousins."

"A wonderful coincidence!" I said, though I would stay in student lodgings. I added an afterthought, alluding to our similar fate: "Our fathers have definite plans."

Michel, who had once visited his cousins in Avignon, described the city to me as one of "massive walls and a hundred towers," though later from my father (who occasionally traveled to that city for business), I learned that the number of towers only added up to thirty-nine. Michel likewise said that Avignon was still under papal control, though no longer the residence of His Holiness. I expressed an interest in seeing the papal palace but my father said it had fallen into disrepair. The return of the Pope to Rome, however, had not diminished Avignon's educational program, considered one of the best in France and only a day's coach ride away from Saint-Rémy.

As Michel and I sat across from each other and talked about the student life ahead, nothing further was said about friendship and its near loss, a topic that does not bear up well under the weight of discussion.

∾

THE SUMMER PASSED hot and sweetly scented with lavender and thyme. Mornings I helped my father in his shop, and Michel studied Latin with his tutor. The long days seemed precious with the knowledge that soon we would leave home. Many restless afternoons we walked through the countryside and talked of how our lives would change. Then one day I devised a game.

"Test your logic on this," I challenged Michel. "Take as your premise a statement about one of our neighbors. Work out the kind of person he was in his youth. What were his hopes, his ideal of love?"

Michel raised his brow in an awakening of interest. The man who came to mind was a greedy baker, someone we both knew well. "Today we see Jules Fenelon at around sixty years of age. From the way he operates his pastry shop, and considering his wife," Michel grinned, both of us thinking that the woman must weigh eighteen stone, "perhaps Fenelon's ideal was to become a purveyor to nobility and provide mountains of delicacies to their guests. But dreams have a way of turning upside down and sideways."

I chuckled at his account of Jules Fenelon, which Michel delivered with mock gravity. Seeing my response he went on to give "histories" of other townspeople. His talent for playing my game seemed surprising at first, for I had never considered Michel as someone with a sense of humor or given to flights of fancy, but when I remarked on this he said, "Such fanciful thinking is logical at its core. Identify a man's present situation, imagine the origin in an earlier time, add a touch of Socratic irony, and you have the humorous effect."

WE SET OUT on the last day of summer, our bundles of clothing and other belongings tucked beneath our seats and in front of us on the carriage floor. I brought along a few volumes of poetry and intended to guard them carefully because the printed editions came dear. Michel also brought a bundle that appeared to be books, judging by sharp corners visible beneath burlap wrapping. I pointed at the shape by way of asking about its contents.

"Some are very old, written on disintegrating vellum, and I would be unable to replace them," he said over the din of carriage wheels biting into the ruts of a dry road. "They belonged to my great-grandfather, then to my grandfather, and now they are mine."

The offhanded way he mentioned the old man re-opened a topic. "I remember that strange day I left you staring at patterns on the ground. Was that connected to the subjects you were studying with him those two years?"

A gust of wind whipped through the coach window. Michel sat silently at first and I feared I had reopened a wound. "Some day I will tell you what happened that afternoon," he said, turning away and squinting into the sun, and then he lowered his voice. "Some day, but only after I learn more about the Mysteries, and only if I know you are sincere. At least I know you are capable of keeping a secret."

I nodded, hoping I looked sincere rather than skeptical and must have succeeded because he went on:

"My family is descended from the Tribe of Issachar, keepers of an ancient and forbidden tradition. Before my birth, when the Jews of Provence were forced to decide between leaving their land or converting to the Church, my forebears relinquished their faith, just as in Israel the Tribe of Issachar long ago chose to remain in comfort among its captors."

"But the teachings you speak of," I interrupted, "they are no longer secret, for surely your grandfather taught you the knowledge handed down to him. What was so secret about ancient history and dead languages?"

"I cannot describe the Mysteries in everyday terms. They are like poetry, for poetry employs symbols; they are like logic, for one idea follows from another just as a conclusion may be implicit in the premise that precedes it."

The coach wheels hit a cavernous rut and sent our belongings sliding. Michel rearranged his things and continued as though there had been no disturbance. "In this secret study I was taught the art of symbols and the linking of hidden truths. I saw in a vision that one day I would discover a grand chain of causes and consequences. That is all I can tell you, for now."

"Did you fathom the old man's secrets?"

"No, I am more perplexed than before. There was so

much to learn and after one year he began to fail, though I asked questions until his last lucid hours. I received only a small portion of the legacy I was promised."

After our talk that day, I often wondered when Michel pored over his grandfather's books or practiced mysterious rites, the nature of which I could only guess. During the first weeks in Avignon I doubt if he had occasion even to unpack his burlap bag, so scarce was our private time.

At first he resided with his cousins, but he complained so much about the noisy, crowded household that within a few weeks he had joined me in student lodgings. Our rigorous schedule started at four in the morning when the proctor roused us from sleep.

The earliest hour was always a blur to me, though Michel seized the darkness with teeth clenched in the cold, his brow set in a determined frown. He jerked on his hose, doublet and black-belted gown and somehow was dressed and downstairs before I even began to pull on my leggings. I managed to find my way down the stairs and out the door, where I stood for a moment along with other students as we made water on the courtyard wall.

After Mass and breakfast of plain hard rolls, the lectures began. The main class of the day was held earliest, when we were still alert. From ten to eleven we engaged in discussion and argument, then lectures occupied us for the remainder of the day.

During the first year, Michel and I attended many

of the same classes. We suffered the discomfort of damp classrooms with our feet tucked into straw that imparted a semblance of warmth in rooms bare except for benches and lectern.

One day while a professor held forth on the subject of Latin declension, I noticed Michel was drawing on a sheet of paper atop his scriptorium. He dipped his sharpened pen into the inkwell then inscribed small figures in the margin, interspersed with an occasional note from the lecture. The figures were so small that when the explorator passed by Michel's bench he saw only the Latin notes in Michel's ordinary handwriting.

I recognized the marginalia as astrological symbols and suspected that he had been studying this unofficially; the subject was part of Avignon's advanced curriculum, for which he was not yet eligible. I wondered why he would give in to such a distraction during a difficult Latin lecture, and later, during our recreation time after supper, I asked him about it.

"Let me ask you a question," he countered. "How do you craft your poetry? When do you compose?"

I replied that I felt compelled to write whenever a phrase arose in my mind; moreover, I found the very urgency of this act fascinating for it seemed to come from another realm, one outside my head.

"Then you have answered your own question, for that applies when I look upon a natal chart or horoscope. At first the task of learning planets and their attributes was tedious, as was mastery of the mathematical techniques, but now that I have begun to accomplish this I often experience what you have described—a flood of ideas."

"For me, sometimes unlikely incidents or objects suddenly give rise to a verse."

"As it is for me. When I enter a labyrinth of symbols at night, insights rise to the surface by day, even during Latin class. For example, if I cast a chart and see Mars located in the Fourth House of domestic matters, I picture the native's temper erupting near the hearth. In this way the hidden messages in the horoscope are revealed."

"Then astrology is related to the symbols you were studying with your grandfather."

"As another branch of the same ancient tree."

AVIGNON WAS ONLY a day's ride from Saint-Rémy, but the stern clerics did not encourage travel home, perhaps to maintain discipline with as little interruption as possible. Nonetheless, Michel and I, like most of our fellow students, did return home for Calendo, as we call Christmas in Provence, and to celebrate the Resurrection at Eastertime.

During my visit home in spring of the year 1521 my father began talking about the draper's trade and assuming I would join him. I had no desire to follow in this business for the world was changing with new books and ideas springing up daily, it seemed. Still, I did not display my lack of interest for fear that he would prematurely make me leave the university. Several of my schoolmates were in a like predicament with heads full of new ideas and fathers clinging to old ones.

This was a time when learning came within reach of merchants' sons who, once they had tasted the writings of Greece and Rome, aspired to achievements other than trading. In Michel's case, it was assumed that he would pursue medical studies, though I knew he was unlikely to follow such a path.

Even before the overflowing banks of the Rhone cut short our studies, this problem came to the fore. Now I had never been as serious a student as Michel, but we did share a talent for memorization, a trick I rarely used since the walled city of Avignon offered subjects more exciting than the scholarly disciplines that comprised the *trivium*. In particular, I was drawn to a certain wine-purveyor's daughter whom I finally succeeded in bedding, though Michel remained indifferent to my accomplishment. On this note of dubious triumph I completed the first year of studies and we returned home.

My homecoming began auspiciously, at least during the first few hours. Upon my arrival, while the carriage horses stamped impatiently and my parcels were being hoisted to the ground, I received embraces and congratulations from my parents and sister. My father was puffed up with pride.

For the dinner celebrating my return and completion of the first year, my mother prepared a feast of lamb in wine and garlic with olive slices shining in the broth like glistening rings. However, I must accept responsibility for a nasty slip in the afternoon's festive mood. After the meal I began to flaunt my knowledge of Greek and Latin poets, and from this display of erudition it was a small step to standing up beside the table and proclaiming my chosen profession.

"Father," I announced in a voice made bold by wine. "I intend to follow in the footsteps of François Villon and practice the profession of poetry, and like him bring fame and honor to our family."

My father leaned forward in his chair ready to dissuade me. "Wait!" I said, raising my hand. "I anticipate your objection. Poetry is not a reliable profession unless one has a wealthy patron, so in order to earn a livelihood I am prepared to seek employment as a tutor."

"Your interest in ancient writings and poetry is merely a passing fashion of our age," he argued. "It seems every young man who can afford an education is determined to dredge up and translate 'lost' writings. Soon there will be a surfeit of tutors and you will be forced to offer your services for a sou."

There was truth in his assessment, for a love of the antique had swept France since the last campaign in Italy. Moreover, it was a pagan inspiration and some day the very literature I hoped to teach might be proscribed by the

Church. If so, I would reap no benefit for my trouble and for my father's expenses of one hundred livres a year in support of my education.

"However," my father said pensively, "if you persist in this infatuation for the written word then perhaps you should apprentice with a printer."

His proposition left me speechless and standing awkwardly in front of my half-consumed dish of lamb. I tried to clear my winey head and consider my position but he was ahead of me.

"I will write to your Uncle Léon. With his considerable influence, I am confident that he will be able to arrange an apprenticeship in Paris." I suspected that the letter had already been sent.

I was neither delighted nor dismayed, for in a haze of youthful optimism I believed other doors would open in welcome to my talents. But this was not all that buoyed my spirits. In that two-year adventure away from home I had discovered another talent. After overcoming an initial shyness, I found I was naturally endowed with a ready geniality that had already earned me unexpected favors. As patronage came my way, obstacles seemed to dissolve. And so, as my father stood before me awaiting a response, I thought: *as long as I am in Paris, surely good fortune will find me.*

When I called upon Michel the next day, I found myself tangled in another confrontation. When I walked in I heard Michel tell his father, "My life would be wasted prescribing tonics." He turned to me. "Alain knows of my devotion to astral studies. Father, with all respect, you have no idea of my ability in what you call 'charlatanry.' My vision is a gift."

His father cut in, "*Bah* to your gift! Your grandfather had a gift. He was a healer of men." Michel's father then proceeded to repeat the story of a poor farmer's son who had been mauled by a boar. We waited patiently as Jaume de Nostredame built up to the final line:

"… and he administered to the boy with such skill that beyond all hope the leg was healed, and the boy grew to be a man who tended his fields, instead of a cripple cowering in the streets. And all this was because of the healing gifts of your grandsire."

Michel sighed as his father added a new ending to the litany. "I expect you to complete the preparation for a degree in medicine at Montpellier. Otherwise you may gaze at the stars from the charity college of Montaigu, where miserable food and lice will aid your meditations."

Michel faced me, and I knew by the defiant set of his mouth and the blade-gray chill of his eyes that his decision was made: Montaigu. I dreaded the consequences. Michel was less robust than I, and the comfort of our childhood in Saint-Rémy had not prepared him for true hardship.

From stories I had heard of the college of Montaigu, where classes were provided for poor but promising students, Avignon was idyllic in comparison. I imagined him hunched over a book in some cheerless cell, refusing to admit error and return home.

I lingered until his father had retired for the night. Hoping to melt Michel's stiff-backed resistance, I suggested that he not risk the future by taking such a rigid stance and offered him the following argument, founded upon my philosophy of survival formulated the day before.

"Accept your father's offer," I advised. "Go to Montpellier and fulfill the medical requirements. At the same time pursue your own studies. It may take longer but your father will not object, and he will not know you are dividing your time, just as he remained unaware of your clandestine studies with your grandfather."

Michel raised his left eyebrow; I had piqued his curiosity. "You say I should devote one day to anatomy and the next to astral delineation?"

"Well, I may have agreed to become a printer's apprentice, but I intend to spend every possible moment composing poetry and mastering my lute. I intend to stretch myself into a printer-poet-musician."

"Then I will be a success with only two mistresses," he said, laughing, "and you will be torn apart by three. " I knew then I had won.

He walked a short distance with me. The hour was late and, with no moon casting light, the streets dark and empty. He spoke with respect about my printer's apprenticeship and recalled the excitement of perusing books and pamphlets in Lyons. I turned in the direction of my home and wished him a restful night's sleep, but after a few steps he called me back.

"I will miss you, my friend," he said. "These have been good years. I am grateful for your help tonight and for evoking the memory of my grandfather. I think he would bless the decision to study medicine while at the same time continuing my search."

"After all," I said, "your grandfather also followed a second and secret path."

WITHIN A FEW MONTHS, Michel was settled in at the medical school at Montpellier, for a while at least, and my father and I had signed our names to a contract with the printer Gabriel Delille.

I traveled to Paris in a coach surrounded by strangers, and though missing my friend I soon caught the scent of independence. Without Michel's absorbing conversations, I would have more time to think for myself, to compose, to practice my lute; without his confining rush to judgment, I would be free to seek the companionship of young women.

The first overnight stop proved a harbinger of adventures to come. The moment I entered the crowded tavern I saw a girl my age, deliciously plump and rosy of cheek. She gave me a knowing smile and conducted me away from other travelers vying for seats, leading me to an alcove where she served my supper in silence, except for a silken brush of her hand as she set out a plate of ham and lentils. I lagged behind until the others left for their rooms and Suzanne had finished her chores. Together we sat at a scrubbed plank table that smelled of soap.

She was lovely but unlettered, and in the dim light of an oil lamp I spun out stories of Avignon and found myself reciting long memorized passages of classical poetry. Before her admiring blue eyes my memory soared. We walked softly up the stairs to my room where I stroked the strings gently to a contented audience of one, and she slept curled against me until sunrise.

Good fortune accompanied me during the journey to Paris, urging on my high spirits and affording safe passage. As our coach neared the city and we began to traverse the outer bridge, I prayed silently to the Virgin: *May this venture bring me a decent life and tender memories as consolation in my later years.*

Then a gloomy notion clouded my prayer as I wondered if the sum of my life would consist of pretty tunes and frivolous recollections, so I retracted the first prayer and before we had completed the bridge crossing I made a firm resolve. I pledged to achieve perfection in the poetic arts, original compositions each better than the one before; I would not squander my days on another poet's lines to win the favor of another impressionable girl.

Despite my sincerity, though, I was to be tormented

with temptations. They began with Monsieur Delille's wife.

Gabriel Delille was a meticulous craftsman and a miser. When I arrived at his home, struck speechless after my first ride through the city, he installed me in an attic room barely large enough for a small pallet of straw, a minuscule chest to hold my clothing, and barely enough remaining floor space to prop the lute on end against my modest collection of books. In order to conserve space I piled one book atop the next in a small leather tower, inconvenient if I needed a book on the bottom. Within this compact arrangement a strip of uncluttered plank flooring led like a dwarf's footpath to the shoulder-high door.

After I had removed road dust with tepid water from a chipped lavatory bowl, I descended the narrow stairs and landed on the ground level, where I heard the rhythmic clash of metal striking against metal. The noise led me through a crude passageway between Delille's home and print shop, which filled the lower story of an adjoining structure.

I expected the press to be smaller, a more compact piece of machinery, perhaps because of the modest size of its product, but before me I saw a hulking construction of black iron. The amazement on my face was plain. Delille laughed and offered me a skimpy mug of wine. "To my new apprentice," he said, tipping the pewter mug and emptying it in one gulp. He grinned slyly and winked a beady eye. "And to your uncle's influence—may it profit us both."

I raised my mug and drained it to the dregs, which

was not difficult for my portion consisted of just that; nevertheless, it was bracing. Delille gestured toward the press. "I think it fitting to drink a cup in her presence. Her forebears crushed grapes, but it took a clever, abstemious man to put a wooden block in place of the grapes, and another clever man to think beyond a single carved block to the casting of separate letters so that type could be broken down and recomposed as another page."

"Remarkable," I mumbled, relishing the wine and impressed by the imposing black machine.

"Your uncle tells me you know nothing of printing," said Delille, "so I'll begin by explaining a few rudimentary points. First, we apply water to the paper, for it increases the absorption of ink and produces a clearer printed page. You see, water is good for something besides irrigating the farmers' fields and washing soiled linen." He shook his head and added, "My wife thinks it beneficial to soak the body, but I regard that as a waste of time."

So far I had only seen his wife briefly, when I first entered the house with dusty baggage in hand, but I did notice immediately that Madame Delille was a handsome woman scarcely older than myself. She modestly remained distant, not only the day of my arrival but for the next several days as Delille taught me first the simpler tasks and then the more complex.

I was quick to learn, mastering the essential techniques and anticipating the day when I would operate the press alone, though Delille insisted that day was far off. Pleasure in my labor had little to do with my impatience. I sought to work one long day alone and print, hopefully by sunset, a page filled with the words of my own verse. I had even picked out a handsome initial decorative letter to grace the first sentence.

But when my first opportunity arrived it was denied. Delille, confined to bed with a severe chill, swore I was not proficient enough to operate the press by myself, nor had he the strength to devise other tasks for me. I was awarded by accident with a day of pure, precious leisure.

An entire day to myself. In my mind I quickly divvied up my windfall of hours as though allocating a pouch of coins, planning time for several coveted projects. First, I would spend the morning composing, then after the mid-day meal I would explore Paris (which I had seen only from my attic window, except for the carriage ride to Delille's). I expected to devote the evening to my lute instead of my usual practice of collapsing exhausted onto my straw bed.

Midway in this tally of precious hours I paused a moment to remember Michel, who by now should be established in the student life of Montpellier. Self-satisfied, I hoped that he, too, had occasional windfalls of time and the resourcefulness to make shrewd use of them. Then I heard a tap on the door and heard Madame Delille say, "A letter has arrived for you."

"A moment." I glanced around the room to see if anything might give offense then opened the low door. She smiled, looking beyond me into the room. My lute caught her fancy and her long-lashed eyes glittered.

She handed me the envelope. "You are a musician?"

Respectfully, I replied, "Yes, Madame." I should have been wary of her interest. Instead I caught the moment much like casting dry twigs on a spark. "I write poems meant to be sung to the instrument."

She assessed the room and wrinkled her nose in disdain, though I could find nothing unpleasant about it. I had made every effort to keep my tiny cell clean.

"What a gloomy little hole he's given you," she said. "Join me downstairs by the fire and I'll listen to your songs. I have nothing special to do today."

I was tempted to answer, "Well, I do have other plans," but I thought it might be prudent to please her. When I could no longer hear her footsteps on the narrow stairs, I removed the sealing wax with my thumb and unfolded Michel's letter:

From Montpellier
Tenth of September
in the year of our Lord 1523

My Dear Alain,
Montpellier is most congenial for a beginning medical student of my temperament, for I have considerable

freedom to observe. Later on my work will be watched more closely. For this reason I keep two sets of notebooks: one to be examined by the doctors as a record of my studies, and a second in which I inscribe my private speculations, about which I will say no more at this time.

Michel went on to describe the city of Montpellier as pleasantly situated on the right bank of the small Lez River, dignified by the presence of a handsome cathedral built some hundred years ago.

He wrote that he had already made the acquaintance of a small group of first-year students who gathered in private to discuss matters discouraged by the Church, among them certain approaches to medical astrology.

Though it was acceptable to delineate natal tendencies, for the planets were assumed to exert an influence overall, lecturing physicians were also Churchmen. One had "corrected" him the first time he phrased his questions in astrological terms. Michel said he had commented that particular day about a patient with a lung disorder and a malevolent aspect to Gemini in the Fourth House. The rector reacted by saying, "Saint Blasius is the patron saint of this organ. You must advise your patients to pray for appropriate intercession: Saint Erasmus for disorders of the abdomen, Saint Apollonia for the teeth and gums, Saints Lucia and Triduana for problems of the eye."

"Besides," another student added sarcastically, under

his breath, "if the treatment fails, then the appropriate saint takes the blame."

Michel recounted this incident, then closed with the often-quoted aphorism attributed to Hippocrates, the father of medicine:

Ars longa, vita brevis...

Now I will give my own transation of this entire saying in the vernacular— his letter continued—for I know that you advocate the use of the living language:

Life is short and Art is long
opportunity fleeting, experiment
dangerous, and judgment difficult

It seems I agree with Hippocrates in all but one point, for I believe experiment is necessary. By experiment our judgment becomes keen.

I smiled at Michel's audacity, presuming to improve upon Hippocrates, though I better understood his reason for guarding his private speculations. I folded the letter again, placed it in my traveling bag, and then remembered that Madame Delille waited for me downstairs. My heart contracted with worry over her intentions. Ah well, I thought, if Michel is right then today's experiment could improve my future judgment.

Madame Delille stirred the smoldering fire with an andiron then asked me to place another log on the hearth. As the pungent bark gave a burst of light to the somber room, she sat down on a cushioned bench and motioned for me to sit on her right. Arranging her skirts beneath her, she subtly edged closer to me until the hem of her gown coverered my left shoe. I placed my lute upon my knee. The notes melded with the sighing hearth as I played a ballad, one familiar enough that she began to hum.

"Now play me a song of your own making," she said. I saw the admiring look but foolishly chose to drink in her attention. My fingers danced across the strings with an excellence of timing and mood that surpassed what I had so far achieved in my best moments.

"You should be a courtier, not an apprentice," she said. "You should be fitted out in velvet, not in cast-off aprons. I can see that your talents are lost here."

Her hand lingered on my arm and my ears rang as I heard her say, "My husband sleeps, and I sent the serving girl on a long errand."

Gabriel Delille remained in bed feverish for three days, and during that time I did not compose nor explore the streets of Paris. When he and I resumed our work at the press on a trebled schedule, with our sleeves rolled up and ink soon caked on our forearms, I often sensed that Françoise Delille was standing behind us. If I dared to turn, her unguarded green eyes sent messages of such unmistakable content that I was sure she sought discovery. I avoided her in self-defense, only to be reprimanded by Delille for being rude to his wife.

"Forgive me," I said, thankful for his ignorance. "I have been intent on completing the work."

But when my eyes met her glance, my body tensed and my face became so miserably flushed that I knew I must take leave before the truth became known. Not only did I risk my livelihood, but also my life, for when he was provoked Delille had the temper of a crazed bear.

I had acquired some knowledge of printing in the past eight months. Surely my uncle with his legendary influence would have other contacts in the trade. But would he care to be bothered with me? Since my arrival, Uncle Léon had not so much as asked after my welfare. Not only was he aloof, but even if I succeeded in winning his sympathy, could he release me from the contract I had signed with Delille?

I sat in my small room that night contemplating my dilemma and vowing to the Virgin in that in future I would keep my hands to myself and my mind on business.

The next morning I requested another day off, but Delille dismissed this wasteful notion, saying curtly, "The press should not be idle," so I resorted to trickery in order to wriggle out of an unsavory situation. I offered a young boy a half-crown to deliver a message to me—from me, but signed Léon Saint-Germain. My Avignon education had left me with an elegant cursive hand, which adapted nicely to several distinctive styles of signature. I had with me Uncle Léon's letter informing me of Delille's offer, and with little effort I copied his signature on a note in which I described him as seriously ill and requesting my bedside presence as his kinsman. Then I added an afterthought: "As you play delicately and with considerable skill, please bring your musical instrument to comfort me." Because the request was from his benefactor, Delille was unlikely to refuse.

Nor did he, and my ruse worked perfectly. Soon after the letter arrived I was out the door and in search of Uncle Léon's home. When I found it, the edifice was no less imposing than I had expected. I sounded the clapper and tried to quell my nervous fidgeting. The first face to appear was a servant boy with a dainty, pinched expression whose eyes opened wide when I said, "Monsieur Saint-Germain expects me. I am his nephew."

"You need no proof but your face," said my uncle, who had been standing out of view just past the door.

He was a handsome man, tall and distinctive in dress, with hair the color of dark wheat, like mine. I was flattered to think that he saw a resemblance. Inside the foyer a marble floor gave further proof of his successful investments in what my father called "questionable banking ventures."

After an exchange of pleasantries about Paris and my

family in Saint-Rémy, I abandoned my manners and bluntly asked if he could arrange for another apprenticeship.

"Perhaps," he said slowly, "but first tell me truthfully of your reason for leaving Delille."

I described the situation, altering it slightly. "If you could arrange another position, I assure you I'll never again risk bringing shame to the family name."

Uneasily, I awaited his response and expected to be chastised, but after what seemed an endless silence he laughed and said, "You seem like no son of my straitlaced brother." Of all unimagined twists! He was delighted by my story, while I had tormented myself with contrition.

Léon assured me I would be freed of my obligations to Delille and that he would secure another position.

"I will inform him I have need of you as aide during my recuperation." He grinned, enjoying the deception.

The same little groom who had opened the door for me now led me to my quarters, and what fine quarters they were in merciful contrast to Delille's musty roomlet.

Large and airy, the room had an armoire of carved oak large enough to contain ten times my wardrobe, along with a tapestry-upholstered chair with arms fashioned after the clawed paws of a mythical beast. The canopied bed was covered with a spread of fabric that must have taken five weavers a year of blinding labor to produce.

That afternoon while my uncle attended to business affairs, I waited in my room idle and pleasantly alone. In dreamy abstraction I gazed out the window, which gave onto a garden bright and aromatic in the spring breeze. In this felicitous yet unfamiliar place, with the scent of crushed mint wafting in from below, I was snared by the first words of a poem.

Barely pausing to adjust the strings, I positioned my lute and strummed a few notes, prompted by an emerging mood. The song grew slowly with hesitant phrases and re-arrangement of notes until my ears told me they were true. At first I sang of Françoise Delille, but the woman soon ceased to be the lady in particular and the woman in my poem assumed another visage. Her eyes no longer glinted with a craving for danger but were trusting and tranquil. Although the lady in my poem was also bound to a man for whom she had no love, fate cancelled the vow of fidelity. I sang of what might have been, transforming the past into a ballad false to memory but true to imagination.

I had just begun the final line and was searching for an unresolved chord when Léon called from outside my door. I set aside the lute and my notations, smoothed my rumpled coat, and followed him down a long hallway.

We entered his library, its walls lined with costly bound volumes. As I breathed in the mingled smells of leather and smoke from the carved fireplace, I felt simulta-neously awed and yet worthy of enjoying the atmosphere of prosperity in which I now found myself.

"Be seated," he said, pointing to a chair. "Now, besides

the distraction of Delille's wife, did my nephew find the printing trade to his liking?"

"No, it was tiresome and dirty."

"So you seek a more inspiring apprenticeship, and what might that be?"

Not wanting to admit that my muse prefers handsome quarters to a garret, I said, "One more demanding of my brains than of my shoulders, one where I do not have to wake up each morning caked in yesterday's grime." But he saw through me.

"Your room is ordinarily reserved for visiting noblemen. Three dukes and one prince have slept in that same bed."

"Forgive me, uncle, I did not mean to presume."

"Perhaps a failing we share," he said, "but you must learn to disguise your desires. Now it so happens that I have something in mind. Of course, as a page your lodgings would be modest but your days and nights would be spent in the undeserved luxury you seem to prefer."

I nodded in assent, holding my breath.

"As my kindred, your appointment to this position would repay me for favors owed. The chains of debt in Paris are unending, and I would exact a fee from you in return. If you accept my offer then you will become my discreet agent within the walls."

In this scheme I would report to Uncle Léon monthly or more often if an occasion arose. His business was lending money, his clients were people highly placed in court, also their relatives and hangers-on. The interest he received may have been, strictly speaking, usurious, but those in need of his services gladly paid a premium in order to access his funds. Since the rates he charged were illegal though not uncommon, if one of his clients could not pay then he had no legal recourse. I would be expected to keep him informed of those who were in or out of favor, since the latter were most likely to cause him a financial loss.

"I will ask nothing to give your conscience unrest," he added, "but your ears will be mine as regards court matters."

Because I thanked him so calmly, he regarded me with curiosity. "You do not seem surprised by this turn of events. Your complacency puzzles me."

I tried not to look smug as I said, "The day I arrived in the city, I had a feeling that Paris would favor me."

Before he dismissed me, Leon outlined his program. He would arrange for instruction in comportment and I would be fitted out with new clothes. I would learn who's who, and about partisan divisions. "Before your duties begin, you will travel as my emissary to deliver a parcel in Carcassonne. Consider the journey as a stage in your training."

This meant I would not be far from home or from Montpellier. "I would like to visit my family and a close friend who is presently studying medicine near Carcassonne," I began.

"Another few days of travel will not matter. I will arrange for your duties to begin in six weeks—but first we must attend to your wardrobe and demeanor. Apply yourself, sharpen your manners, then travel as a nobleman." He paused and considered my appearance. "We have much work ahead of us; paring away two layers, the student and the printer's apprentice."

On the third day, he called me back to his library. "Tell me, Alain," he began, "what are your sentiments on the subject of, shall we say, divergent religious sects?"

I gave an evasive reply. "While I was a student, I listened to stories of abuses that led to the rise of renegade religious groups." I had heard stories of priests who cohabit with nuns in secret underground passageways, and of bishops who sell dispensations for gold. "And yet," I added, "in Saint-Rémy the Churchmen were kind and sincere. In Avignon I found them learned and devout."

I mentioned the printed tracts condemning the Church that circulated clandestinely in Avignon and students who stood in clusters and discussed them. "I do not know what to believe," I said. "You place me in an awkward position, Uncle. You must have an interest in the old Church or in the new movement, but I cannot tell which.'"

"Of course I attend Mass and I receive Holy Communion, because it is politic to do so."

"Then your piety is a matter of convenience."

"As it is for many of us, and you may draw this conclusion if you wish. But we will discuss it no further today. Your task is to gather information impartially as though I am a devout Churchman and also a supporter of the reformers. Listen for rumors. Our King shifts his policies, so does the court, and so must I."

Thus began my lesson in polity and court intrigue. Léon said he doubted if the King would venture far from the Church, for by doing so he had little to gain. For unlike his contemporary Henry VIII of England, François had papal consent to appoint bishops and abbots, which meant payment and power were already in his hands. But my uncle saw no end to the protestant movement, so strong was its momentum and so varied its followers. "Moreover," he said, "who knows which way the wind will blow once the Dauphin is anointed king."

"But he is only a boy," I said, wondering how many rulers my uncle intended to outlive.

"Perhaps that will happen in many years or a few. I am always packed and ready for change, and when it occurs I alter my position; a realignment of gesture and phrase, a few coins spread in the right direction, and the future is once again secure."

"Until the next upheaval."

"I find such uncertainty no encumbrance to living fully. It goads me on to a lively old age."

The groom reappeared to refresh our wine cups. Intentionally, no doubt, he spilled a few drops on my wrinkled doublet. Thinking his apology insincere, I glowered at him until he departed.

With our privacy restored, Uncle Léon told me about the King's lavish spending. With a treasury near bankruptcy, François had sworn to limit his excesses in new building construction, yet rumors spread that another campaign might be advanced into Italy for the fattening of French coffers and the enhancement of the King's magnificence.

By now I understood that I was to make rumors my business. Names and family connections swam in my head. Léon assured me they would soon become clear, but the day's discussion left me tired and perplexed. I was to disregard no one, for he explained that influence is found in both bedchamber and council chamber.

He urged me to observe the friendships and enmities of the family de Guise, lords of the duchy of Lorraine. "You will see them often in court," he advised. "Learn to read their manner as though you were following a map, for in their direction may lie the future of France and the fate of the line of the Valois.

"At first, you will report details I already know," he continued. "On the basis of these early reports, I will be in a position to appraise your perception and judgment. Soon you will outdistance my own ready information, for I am here and you will be inside the walls."

At the close of my last lesson he handed me a purse, and I was told a servant would escort me on my journey.

"Do not regard him as a comrade," said my uncle, "for he is your inferior. When you enter royal service you should retain a nobleman's air. The dignity of your position demands it." I thought of his arrogant little groom. "Remember," he said finally, "you too have been served."

I departed early the following morning, while the river's mist clung to the towers of Notre Dame, clad in a fine new suit of bottle-green velvet trimmed with black braid and brass buttons.

My restive gray mare became more manageable once we had turned onto country roads, and at my side rode a tired old servant named Jacques, sleepily mounted on a gelded roan.

The first day I was uncomfortable with this arrangement; for one thing, it was my natural tendency to converse but Léon had instructed me to avoid familiarity. Jacques and I rode in a silence broken only by hoof beats and bird song. After our stop at a roadhouse near Montargis, I came to accept my time-withered escort and appreciate his gentle care of the horses and fastidious attendance to my garments. With his wrinkled hand and a brush he could restore luster to a horse's coat or a dusty riding cloak.

A few days later we entered the city of Montpellier and made our lodgings in a hostelry adjacent to the college, an inn renowned for fairly clean linen and a nightly fare of hearty stew. I left Jacques at the inn with instructions to unpack my parcels; meanwhile, I set out for the college of medicine in hopes that, once I had arrived, someone would direct me to Michel de Nostredame.

Beyond a fortified door with a pair of heavy iron pulls the bustle of Montpellier subsided and I found myself standing in a damp, musty hallway. From a nearby room a droning professorial voice held forth on the subject of fractures. My eyes, now accustomed to the muted light, looked up the dim corridor and counted a dozen lecture halls. I was dejected. The trip had been tiring, but throughout I had bolstered my spirits by anticipating the moment when I would see my friend. I had failed to consider the problem of locating him.

The droning voice ceased, and in a great rustle of black robes the students spilled through doorways and into the hall where I waited. I searched preoccupied faces for the familiar one—or would it be? Less than a year had passed, but I had changed from a round-cheeked student in rumpled clothes with a shy smile to a soon-to-become royal attendant in velvet livery with an increasingly bold countenance and a dark blond beard now grown thick though I kept it in trim.

The youths with their dark robes and full unkempt beards looked like a unified mass of wool and whiskers as they walked down the passageway. Thinking that surely Michel had distinguished himself I supposed I had only to ask, and in a way events proved me right.

A professor walked past, cutting a swath through

the crowd of young people. To catch his attention I spoke up. Following my uncle's advice, I assumed what I thought simulated a nobleman's air, and could sense by the professor's deference that he judged me of high birth.

"I seek a student named Michel de Nostredame." His glance lingered on my fancy brass collar button.

"If you attend my next lecture you will find him, for he never misses a word or an opportunity to interrupt and argue for his unorthodox notions."

He peered at me warily. "May I inquire about your interest in him?"

"I am visiting Montpellier on court matters," I lied.

The doctor said hastily, "I did not intend to disparage the young man, for he is an unusual student. A bit rebellious perhaps, but when he embarks upon his own practice he will discover that traditional methods are best, most comforting to the patient and most comfortable for the physician." He caressed his ruby ring. "My next lecture begins at the eleventh hour."

And at the eleventh hour Michel appeared in the hallway. He had a tangled dark beard and in most respects was indistinguishable from the others, but what caught my eye was not the Michel I remembered but the imprint of his father's stern visage. He identified me at once, and I wondered if news had spread that a smart courtier had asked for him. Clearly I stood out against the run of indifferently clad students and red-robed professors.

"Welcome to Montpellier," he said dryly. "Our modest town must seem an uneventful place after Paris." He scrutinized my costume. "I see you are prosperous. A printer's apprentice must be well compensated these days."

How typically Michel, I thought, making me feel like a peacock in a convent. I mumbled an apology for my discordant dress, and explained that I was no longer apprentice to a printer but soon to begin duties in the Valois court, thanks to Léon's arrangements.

"Congratulations," said Michel with thinly concealed scorn. This galled me to protest, "Do superficial details matter so greatly to you?"

Michel smiled. "Well, my dear poet, you force me to admit that I am pleased to see you. We were always as far apart as the midheaven and nadir."

"As you once summed it up, I was born under the light of the sun and you under the gloom of Saturn. How goes it, then, with your study of the stars?"

"I have managed to retain what I learned in Avignon, no thanks to your specious scheme. I spend most of my time studying medicine, rare moments on astral studies, by which time I am desperate for my sliver of sleep."

"No wonder you seem grim. No time for pleasure."

"Or any other vice," he said curtly.

The anatomy lecture was about to begin and he assured me the professor would not object to my visit. We thus concluded our conversation on a strained note and followed other students into the lecture hall, taking two remaining seats on a bench toward the rear. An anatomical diagram rested on a tripod in front of the class in the revered space where a moment later the professor entered to applause and cries of "*Vivat!*"

For a tedious hour the eminent doctor shuffled his notes and tapped out examples on the chart with a long black pointer. I tried to pay attention out of courtesy but the lines denoting musculature and viscera were a tangle to my untrained eye. I confessed this to Michel after the lecture, to account for my uncontrollable yawning, while we strolled toward the Grey Swan for our midday meal.

"An anatomical rendering is inadequate compared to real work with a cadaver," he said, telling me that during the last year when he was still a new student he had been quite outspoken on the matter of dissection, but that he wasted his voice. "They teach us to debate a fine point as though this was the goal of education. I am here to learn the physician's art and sometimes I think Montpellier is nothing but an impediment. No matter, though, for this exercise in irrelevance will soon end." I suggested that his understanding could not be hindered by studying anatomy and the signs of illness.

"Formulas and rules. Greater vision is needed in the art of healing to see where the rules of medicine and symbols either meet or diverge."

We walked toward the river as autumn sun filtered

through the trees and cast dappled shadows on our path. "This is not the most direct route," said Michel, "but I favor the autumn months when every color of nature seems in a state of transformation. The view is best from the river's edge. I come here often to unwind my thoughts."

I could appreciate how the gently flowing current and the vista of the city behind us might soothe the overwrought mind of someone whose conflicting thoughts required two separate notebooks.

We descended a stone stairway to what would have been in springtime a grassy bank. Now it was already dry and prickly to sit on, but I imagined it greened with a girl in arm's reach and a bottle of wine cooling nearby in the reeds. The afternoon sun and lack of shade prompted Michel to remove his heavy outer robe, disclosing a thinner woolen garment beneath and a largish pouch hanging from a belt at his hip. He saw my curiosity and said, "I will show you my new treasure, an astrolabe. Have you ever seen one?"

I admitted I had not and thought such instruments were used by seamen, but apparently they had some astrological application as well.

Michel pulled it out and I saw that one of its features was a metal disk, and on its face was another inlaid disk. A single diametrical rule or indicator intersected the two circles. He turned it over and on the back I saw a map of the constellations.

"These indicators show the positions of the stars relative to one another and in relation to the sun. With this table I can calculate the planetary aspects on any given day. By rotating this arm I can read from the line of coincidence the time of day."

I held it up and nodded with admiration, though the astrolabe offered me no useful information. Perhaps it took several lessons to manipulate it correctly. It was a handsome object, though, with a clever fretwork design around its perimeter.

"Now that you have seen my meditation place and my new device, I will take you to supper at the Grey Swan."

INSIDE THE HOSTELRY the air was redolent of the aroma of savory broth. We seated ourselves at a crowded table, its surface scarred by decades of carving knives. Michel signaled to the innkeeper, who soon placed steaming bowls of beef and root vegetables in front of us.

"Are you still penning your poetry?" Michel asked between mouthfuls as he sopped up the last dabs of broth in chunks of bread while I did the same.

"Not as often as I had hoped, but I am satisfied with a few verses. I copied one from my journal for you, though perhaps it is a misnomer to call it a journal since I do not write in it daily. The material is nonetheless culled from circumstances that could be reconstructed by the calendar."

I took a slim roll of parchment from my doublet; on it I had copied in my best cursive script the love poem transfigured from my memory of Françoise Delille. Michel unrolled the page and read my quatrain.

"Eloquent, I grant, but I cannot commend you for glorifying illicit love."

I had expected such a reaction from this black-robed young man who had never seen Paris and was sheltered from the delights of what, to me, represented the real world. Never infatuated by a flesh and blood woman, he would miss the point of anyone's love poem.

"A fair objection." I could afford to give in, convinced of the value of my work. Still, his respect was important to me. Then from memory I began to recite another verse, one I had written in honor of Michel's Platonic ideals:

> *The heart untouched waits nearest God*
> *Until the gift of love is given at last*
> *In your eyes I see a mirror of my gaze*
> *Together in His sight is our love blessed.*

"Needs a bit of polish, but the sentiment shines through," he said with a half smile. "I suspect that you are not so reprobate as you like to seem, but I caution against mistaking the shadows in Plato's cave for reality. That is no way to care for your soul."

Seeing an opening for one of my pressing questions I began, "It seems to me the souls of entire countries are at stake, with the Church increasingly at odds with the Reformers. Does this amount to theological hair-splitting, or do you think the reformers' condemnation of the Catholic Church is warranted?"

He sidestepped my question. "The Church has endured for almost two thousand years and will endure for millenia."

"A pronouncement fit for the pulpit," I said, then spliced on an opinion of Uncle Léon's. "Some think the Church will be supplanted by a new order in our lifetime."

It later occurred to me that Michel might have spoken so formulaically in support of the Church as a safeguard. Did he speak in public in a pious voice because he feared to be known as the descendent of Hebrews, or to mask his interest in what some called paganism or black arts?

"Tell me of your own faith," I said. "You once told me insights from the study of the stars were more beneficial to mankind than a thousand repetitions of the Mass."

"I believe the Church is catholic or universal because it has absorbed the teachings of the Hebrews, the Greeks, and secret sects that existed in ancient times." He lowered his voice. "This does not undermine my faith but strengthens it, for my belief rests not in a god or gods but in the symbols that lead us to understanding. The Church with its calendar of rites and saints satisfies the souls of most men. To me, the Church is a childhood home I must leave to wander."

With my curiosity satisfied and to avoid a theological discussion for which I was ill prepared, I returned to the topic of the hour. "How can you give up this fine stew even for a few weeks?" Lenten season with its meatless restrictions was soon to begin.

"I am accustomed to fasting and not only on days prescribed by the Church," he said. "It frees me from the distractions of mealtime and focuses my concentration."

When I speculated that I would benefit from improved concentration, he disagreed. "My style of inward concentration would not suit you. Just the opposite. You've chosen the way of intrigue and spying on others, or this is my impression of your new life in the Valois court."

"I object to your terms," I said, though he was right. Upon my return to Paris my assignment would be assisting the tutor for the two princes, and I was concerned that serving as attendant to children placed me in a poor position for gathering information. I was embarrassed about the trivial nature of my duties. Time would prove me wrong.

"No doubt you will have much to tell your uncle," Michel ventured. "We even overhear rumors in Montpellier, such as hearsay in the hallways that the Duke of Bourbon may attempt to seize Provence."

"Rumors trade cheaply and far."

"I have dreams that seem as vague as rumors," he said. "Often I wake with a feeling of certainty, though the meaning of the dream remains unclear. I record details in my notebooks in the middle of the night, but when I look at my own words in the light of morning, I have no idea of why the dream was so convincing."

"My midnight verses often make for strange reading." Michel had no idea of how bawdy these could be.

"Perhaps you have not discovered your true poetic subject," he said. By now we were nearing the river again on our way back to where I had left Jacques waiting to resume our journey. "Today you are concerned with private moments and portraits of love. In your new position you will be surrounded by talk of military campaigns and struggles for power. You will widen your vista," Michel said with a gesture toward the river flowing past us.

I saw a new glimmer in his eyes as he went on. "You might write an epic poem spanning centuries, a work of real consequence."

Never would I be inspired to do so, of course, and I only realized many years later that he took his own advice to heart. Or maybe he had a premonition of a sweeping work to come but remained unclear about its authorship. In any case, our time together in Montpellier was brief.

As we parted that day I said, "Next time we meet, you will be dressed in the four-pointed hat and wear the physician's ring."

He parried: "And you, no doubt, will be wearing a different shade of velvet."

MY RETURN TO PARIS was blighted by foul weather. While riding into heavy rains on a barren stretch of road, my horse lost a shoe in the muck and I had to dismount. If traveling alone I would have slogged along on foot, but because Jacques was with me I shared his roan and the incident caused little delay except a stop at the village smith.

Storm clouds had moved south by the time we arrived back at my uncle's home, and I welcomed the next day anticipating my new role. That morning I chose a brown velvet tunic and matching hose. Léon's driver transported me by carriage to Les Tournelles with the assurance that I was expected.

No doubt great favors were owed to my uncle, for unlike me my fellow attendants were all of noble birth, and the only flawed moment of the first day came when someone asked how a nobody like me came into such a choice position. Mention of Léon Saint-Germain brought an immediate apology and that night a flask of cognac appeared anonymously in my room.

The young Dauphin was only six years old, but as I watched him playing in the nursery I thought: Someday this runny nosed child will be King and here I am, amid assorted playthings and nurses, tending to his needs. I judged that my uncle would want me to become indispensable, and I did so. I charmed the nannies and soon came to be regarded by Queen Claude as the most conscientious of attendants.

Proudly, I said this to Leon at our next meeting.

"Because she is Queen you ascribe power to her, but have you noticed how rarely the King is seen with her?"

"I thought he was busy with his military advisers. There is all the trouble over Provence."

"Where are you keeping your ears? The King is devoted to his mistress, Madame de Chateaubriant, and before her there was another woman. Get yourself in the lady's good graces and do not spend all your charm on the nannies and Queen Claude."

"But what of the children?" I interrupted. "Surely I should cultivate the Dauphin's affection above all others."

"If he succeeds to the throne while in his minority then Queen Claude will be regent and she will be controlled by François's counselors. You would be wise to ingratiate yourself with them too. If the Dauphin were to die, Henri would inherit the throne."

I followed my uncle's advice and divided my attention between both children, also looking for other favors to dispense. The routine of my days became more complex. I found my eyes darting about constantly to see who passed through the hallways. Some nights my dreams jangled with overheard conversations.

Fostering the affections of both the Dauphin and young Henri was no chore, for the children were amiable. The Dauphin had inherited the King's easy manner and his love of entertainment, while Henri was quieter but a contented child who doted on his mother. I found that I favored him, though he was twice removed from the throne. During that year when a third prince was born, I decided to focus my affection on the two eldest; later, my instincts proved correct.

AFTER I HAD BEEN IN COURT only a few months, a military debacle occurred with repercussions for many years. The Duke of Bourbon attempted to seize Provence, but the campaign failed and his troops were driven away by our King's army. In the glow of victory and in retaliation against Emperor Charles of Spain, who had supported the Duke's campaign, our King led his army into Milan.

His next venture proved a disaster. In the battle of Pavia, our soldiers suffered a shameful defeat; worse, and in a monstrous turn of events, the King was captured and subsequently held prisoner in Madrid.

Futile negotiations followed, with terms of prime importance being the release of a captive sovereign who, at one point due to illness and exhaustion, was on the verge of death.

During those uncertain months the court was neither gay nor bristling with information to relay to my uncle. All factions were unified in their concern for the King. In his absence his mother, the Queen Mother Louise, ruled. She was a lady who couldn't be charmed. But I was young, I reminded myself, and when this gloomy period had passed and a treaty was at last ratified, the brilliant life of the court would resume.

In the endless hot months when Paris sweltered, the privileged residents of Les Tournelles sought refuge in the chateau at Blois where fresh breezes blew across vast fields of blossoms cooled by the River Loire. As second tutor to the children I was included in the entourage, and it was at Blois that I came to understand the King's passion for architecture. In the sculpted stonework of the country chateau there were a thousand details to savor. The dominant theme repeated throughout the summer palace, appearing on mantels and in cornices, was the salamander, the King's own device. Its presence offered reassurance, for the salamander is believed to rise from flames unscathed, and so, we prayed, would he.

Times were tense while awaiting his return, and other ominous news reached the countryside where we carried on a dispirited summer routine. A plague had descended on my homeland, the south of France.

I received a letter from Michel late in that year of 1525. Judging by the date he had inscribed at the top of the letter, which was May 13, I knew many months had passed since he composed it, and more before it was delivered into my hands.

At first I wondered why he had chosen me for this unburdening, but had I been faced with such terrible sights and the chance of never seeing family or friends again, perhaps I would wish to leave an account with someone. Only a fragment of his original letter remains.

My Dear Alain,

You will be relieved to know that Saint-Rémy has had little incidence of the pestilence, and your family and mine remain in good health. After your visit to Montpellier I left the college without completing my degree when I heard *le charbon* had stricken the regions of Provence and Languedoc, and when I learned that physicians were abandoning the helpless inhabitants.

In Béziers, the first town where I offered my assistance, I was deceived by the apparent mildness of the scourge, though after I resumed my journey I soon witnessed the plague in its full horror.

When he entered the city gates of Béziers, he later told me, he saw no sign of the pestilence. People strolled the streets, seemingly concerned only with the day's price of almonds, olive oil, or other produce. Shutters of shop fronts stood open and tradesmen busied themselves pleasing customers. He paused before a barber's stall where the barber was removing a towel from a ruddy-faced client. Michel had intended to have a delousing before leaving Montpellier and indicated to the barber that he wished to be next. A small dog, mascot of the shop, sniffed Michel's boots.

"Your business thrives," Michel observed, removing

his hat. By its distinctive shape, the barber knew this customer was a physician though still in training; by the unfamiliarity of Michel's face, he knew that the man he was about to groom was not a local resident.

"You would be a visiting doctor from Montpellier, I'll wager." He sharpened his razor and remarked, "I see no need for extra medics in Béziers. Between the doctors and me we keep our people fit. Of course, there's a kind of simple pox going about lately, but those who get it are up and around within a day."

Michel's errand of mercy, undertaken with such urgency, now seemed unnecessary. "I will need lodging, at least. Could you recommend a room?"

"I'll trim and delouse your hair and beard and put you up in my house, all for a fair charge."

The barber had correctly gauged the disease. In Béziers it was mild though widespread and a patient's pustules quickly subsided. This time Michel had occasion to treat only a few such cases, for his youth and the absence of a ring signifying that he had obtained the certificate led the older doctors to regard him as an apprentice.

He was told to apply a splint to a broken arm and asked to carry orders to the apothecary. Only once did he rankle when a physician told him to cauterize a gunshot wound. Michel refused, saying his method was to treat it with herbal dressings, and if the doctor wished to cauterize the patient then he could do it himself.

At the end of a month's stay in Béziers, Michel paid the balance owed for his lodging, and as he left he happened to mention to the barber his plan to take his mule and ride to Narbonne, where news had reached him there was greater need for his help.

"We have closed the gates to those who arrive from that city," said the barber. "I would not go there, if I were you."

MICHEL HARDLY KNEW what to expect when he arrived at the walled city, for Béziers had shown him the ravages of the disease writ small. Soon he would see torsos covered in pustules or buboes, severe cases accompanied by diarrhea, and lungs filled with fluid so each cough sounded like a death rattle until a final convulsion proved it true.

Yet in his idealism, Michel was confident that he would serve the sick and ease their suffering; for his part, he was well fed, rested, strong, and he entertained no thought that he also might succumb. But after the day's ride, when he arrived in Narbonne, he faced a sight that almost crushed his resolve: A festering death cart rumbled past, conveying a pile of corpses to the pit graves outside the walled city Bodies jostled about when one of the cartwheels struck a stone. Arms and legs askew, four corpses tumbled out and landed in a foul tangle directly in front of him.

Shaken by this omen, he entered Narbonne where inside the gate he asked a disheveled stranger where lodgings might be found.

"Another doctor?" The man spat, then clutched Michel's cloak. "Do you exorcise demons? Can you change a man's destiny?" He gaped, his mouth a foul smelling hole picked with broken teeth. Michel shoved him aside and broke free of his grasp, but the accusing voice pursued Michel as he walked up the street. He tried to make sense of the man's words, assuming that he must be crazed with grief, blaming some physician for the loss of a brother, wife or child.

From an open doorway a younger man appeared, calling for help. Michel nodded in assent, and as he stooped to enter the low doorway he immediately recognized the symptoms. The woman lay on a linen sheet, livid red sores protruding from her pale skin. As Michel raised the sheet and inspected the swollen glands, she stared at him with terrified eyes, for the disease was in a stage of progression that still yielded full consciousness.

Her husband knelt at the bedside. "The doctor is here and I promise you will be healed," he whispered. The husband's vow rendered Michel immobile as his eyes ranged over the woman's body, knowing that he could lance her sores, but unless he could devise some other treatment the husband's prayers were her best hope.

Then a clarity of mind came upon Michel and he noticed the features of the woman's face; her damp hairline, the limp brown hair pushed back from her brow and the gentle curve of her chin, reminiscent of a pale lunar orb. So compelling was the image that he asked the young husband if his wife would celebrate her birthday in July.

"Yes," he replied, "and God willing she will be twenty."

Michel's question assumed uncanny information, but the man was so distraught that he did not think it odd for this physician to speculate about her month of birth.

Child of the moon and twenty. Knowing the position of her sun, and recalling the positions of the two slower moving planets, to this formula he added the more rapidly transiting orbs of Moon, Mercury, Mars, and Venus, and made calculations in his head. With a leap from the star-patterns in his memory, he concluded that a concoction of two herbs might help her. He used no medical axioms from Montpellier for guidance, nor had he time for more accurate mathematical calculations on which to base his procedure, but as he lanced and cleared the abscesses he read her body like the most lucid of diagrams.

The young medic handed the bloody strips of linen to the husband, who obeyed the instruction to throw them into the hearth where flames turned cloth to ash. "I must find an apothecary," Michel said.

"One remains open. His shop is seventh on the row."

"I cannot help others for long if I do not have somewhere to sleep." Exhausted from the ride and by being accosted by the madman, Michel's words sounded harsh.

"You will pass an inn on the way to the apothecary,"

said the man, "but first return with the medicine." With a despairing look, the husband watched the departure of a physician who left behind a patient now in greater agony than before.

Michel returned in the early evening, when by candlelight in the darkened room he tipped a cup to the woman's cracked lips. Time and again he forced her to drink until, when she was unable to drink more, he left the half-filled jar to be given to her throughout the night.

At the inn he fell upon his bed after swallowing a few bites of bread and a dish of broth, exhausted from the day's ordeal. He craved sleep yet fought it, for he had tended to only one patient while hundreds needed his help. Their imagined moans and cries pursued him even after he fell into a restless sleep.

That night Michel dreamed he possessed a wonderful hound, a fine and loyal creature of clear eye and glossy coat. But one morning as he went to feed it, he saw with horror that the sleek body had turned into a transparent and shimmering, sweat filmed substance. Though the dog lived it was unaware of his presence. Michel knew with a chill of certainty that this eerie state was a precursor of death.

He woke from the dream to find that the sun had long since risen above the horizon. Through the glazed window he saw the half-timbered buildings of Narbonne and remembered the immensity of his task. They waited for him, dozens of victims within a few steps of this inn and hundreds all told, for the few doctors who remained in town had barricaded themselves in their homes and refused to touch any victim stricken by the plague.

Michel hurriedly ate a bowl of porridge and hastened to tend to his patient. After the ominous dream, he feared finding the boils swollen with poison, the patient unconscious and on the brink of death, but when the husband greeted Michel at the door his face was haggard yet beaming. During the night the inflamed abscesses had receded, and after much feverish tossing the woman slept deeply until morning, when she woke and requested food.

"I knew she would not desert me and our children," the husband said as if his faith had made it so. Examining his patient and recalling her recent dire condition, the doctor confirmed that the crisis was over. Cautiously, he reminded the husband that it would take weeks of rest before his wife would fully recover. After Michel took his leave, he devoted a silent moment to amazement and thanksgiving, for the direful dream was only an expression of his fears and not a prophecy—at least not on that day.

He treated his next several patients with equal success. He no longer inquired about the patient's nativity to devise a specific treatment, for his intuition became infallible in such matters and his cures succeeded in the most extreme cases. But such success aroused the jealousy of the few physicians who had not abandoned their patients, or those who had abandoned them and now faced the indignity of having them cured by this itinerant and not even fully-fledged doctor. They could not deny the effectiveness of Michel's treatments so they turned their attack to a condemnation of his unorthodox practices.

As Michel worked with his patients, he noticed countless variations in the symptoms of the same disease; through his observations and experiments he found the correlation between healing herbs and planetary influence of increasing interest. Noticing his fascination, the apothecary who had first aided him in making his decoctions discreetly introduced Michel to a frail old man who resided in a tiny room behind a woolen shop. His name was Simon LeCler, a nominally Christian Jew.

In Simon's windowless room, which had the advantage of not being visible from the street, Michel resumed his study of the esoteric teachings of the Kabbalah. On his first visit to LeCler's home he saw on the walls of this secret academy a painted scroll, yellowed with age, portraying the Tree of Life, the tree his grandfather had described to him so many years ago. Within his heart he still carried his grandfather's secret teachings, and now in a tiny room behind a woolen shop he became reacquainted with the mysterious tree depicted on parchment, its sacred branches with the mystic letters of creation at the terminus of each limb.

The first night Michel arrived shortly after sunset. A young man who introduced himself as Simon LeCler's son handed him a small rush mat. Legs folded beneath him, Michel took his place along with four other men who sat on the bare floor. The table on which Simon stacked his bolts of wool was pushed to a far corner. Against the wall, the tailor sat on a rush mat, eyes closed. After a long silence he spoke:

"*En Soph* fills and encloses the universe. As He is boundless, the mind cannot contain Him. From His being, the ten *Sephiroth* emanate like rays from the sun. The visible is a measure of the invisible; it proceeds by analogy from the known to the unknown. Each fragment of nature, each part of the body, corresponds to a portion of the unseen universe. It is to see more clearly this Oneness that we are gathered here tonight."

Afterward, Michel lingered to preserve the sense of awe engulfing him as he sat in candlelight on the rush mat. In a few words this teacher had explained the encompassing natural order that Michel had discovered independently through his healing. He was not alone, nor was he mad; others had seen what he had seen and their vision was recorded long before his birth. He knew his mission was to rediscover secrets dating back to the earliest memories of mankind.

Each night when he left his last patient, Michel went to study with Simon LeCler. For a few hours, the suffering he had witnessed during the day was forgotten. But his apprenticeship would last only a few weeks before threats against his life forced Michel to return to the road.

ONE DAY WHILE he was spooning a pungent decoction of bay and poppy seed into the thin lips of an elderly woman, a physician in red robes entered the patient's home. He stood quietly, assessing Michel's procedures.

"You there," he said, "by what license do you practice medicine?"

"I have been tending your own neglected patients, but it may relieve your conscience to know that I studied medicine at Montpellier." He did not add that he had been asked to leave before completing his degree because of his unusual practices.

"We are pleased to know that at least you did not conjure your skills from beneath a hedge," he said, snatching the jar from Michel's hand and sniffing its contents. "I understand you do not administer geysers nor examine the patient's urine before prescribing these concoctions."

"I find little merit in listening to the pulse, nor in judging by paltry piss," Michel replied.

The doctor thrust his shoulders back, turned and stalked from the room, pausing in the doorway to add with a sly smile: "I speak for the physicians in Narbonne. Your success is due to luck or witchcraft, and for the second you could burn. There are now a dozen of us ready to tend those suffering from the pestilence and your services are not wanted here. Leave by tomorrow or we will tell the authorities that you are a practitioner of the black arts."

That night when Michel walked toward Simon LeCler's room, a hooded man followed close behind him. With defiant pleasure, Michel led him on a labyrinthine walk, making several detours through winding alleyways and once strolling in a full circle around a cluster of buildings. When he returned to his starting point, he saw that the stranger was still behind him, the gray hood pulled low over his forehead. At one point in the night walk, Michel passed the familiar tailor's shop but never slowed his pace. He passed the windowless wall but could not pause without endangering his teacher. The next day he took leave of Narbonne without paying his respects to LeCler, though the lessons of the luminous Tree of Life would remain with him always.

The details of Michel's letter cast me into a melancholy state, though I was relieved to hear that my family was safe for I had not seen them for some time. But I was soon to become even more despondent when informed of a journey required by my service to the King.

The events preceding it gave me no warning.

Shortly after the New Year of 1526 a treaty was ratified between the King and his Spanish captor, though the terms of the agreement were disheartening.

Among other losses of territory, my native Provence would revert to the status of an independent state and I feared my position in court might be jeopardized. But I worried needlessly, for it turned out that the treaty would never go into effect.

Behind the elaborate negotiations carried on in Madrid was this bit of maneuvering: Like a mouse in the woodwork, our ruler had shrewdly relayed a message six months before through his sister Marguerite, who was the only person permitted to visit him during his grave illness.

The document declared that any treaty which the King might sign in captivity was null and void as contracted under duress. Pope Clement sanctified this artful dodge, and while the French parliament was apprised of this, the populace was not to know until the King's release had been secured. This was no simple feat, for a cruel trap lay ahead.

Charles had agreed to release his captive on the King's word, but as a guarantee Charles demanded two royal sons as hostages. Upon hearing this François said, "What good is a King without a kingdom?" and surrendered his sons.

This agreement, for me, meant an apprenticeship in exile. I had shown devotion to the Dauphin and young Henri, so now I was told to accompany the children to Spain. The Queen Mother Louise was no tyrant and I was at will to refuse, but without prompting from Uncle Léon, I sensed that in some future time my sacrifice would be repaid. Had I known the duration of our exile—but of course I could not, and so, unaware of the our King's plan to break the treaty, I trusted that the Spanish would treat two princes and their attendant with all possible courtesy and that before long we would all be home once again.

On the day of our departure, scores of brightly dressed courtiers comprising our traveling party wore such varicolored costumes one might call it making a mockery of festivity. Nature, however, reflected the somber honesty of that gray morning in March when we left Paris on the journey to a town in France at the edge of the detested Spanish border.

We traveled overland slowly, my horse following a litter bearing the two princes. The landscape offered little diversion, but once when a handsome stag appeared on a nearby hillock, I called out to Henri (who loved the hunt), "Look—pull aside the curtain!" His small, frightened face emerged from behind the drape, dark eyes disclosing no emotion. In a moment he had slumped back in his seat again and did not look out until we arrived at the next resting place. For young Henri there was no disguising this journey as an outing.

In a few days we reached the crossing where the princes rested within tents while attendants who would soon return to Paris began preparation for the King's release. The Dauphin was restless with excitement at the prospect of seeing his father for the first time in two years; he had willingly accepted the role of hostage so that his father might continue a sovereignty that some day would be his.

Henri seemed indifferent to his father's reappearance.

Now a sullen seven years of age, Henri had become more withdrawn over the past two years, which many people attributed to the death of his mother, Queen Claude. While she had lived, the boy depended on her quiet strength. That night on the border he stared across the river and grimly awaited tomorrow's exchange, two boys for their royal sire.

We huddled in the river barge as the bargemen thrust their poles into the sand, sending the craft gliding away from the bank. I saw on the Spanish shore what appeared to be our reflection across the blue-green expanse. The river remained a mirror until the distance between the twin barges diminished and the enemy flag came sharply into view. There, in the center of the river, within hands' reach of each other, the two barges passed.

The King gazed helplessly at us, his eyes sunken and dark from recent illness. He called to me as we neared each other mid-river, "Take care of my sons," then to the pair, "I will come back for you soon." In the mingling of uncaring waves he could not hear the two boys who cried out as their father shrank to a speck on the opposite bank.

I LIKE TO THINK that my presence provided some consolation to the children during our captivity. The first day in Madrid, when Spanish guards locked us into large but dreary rooms, I assessed our surroundings and set about at once to amuse the princes, hoping to raise their poor spirits and make the time pass quickly.

Though taught the saintly value of sacrifice, I never intended to become a saint. Quite the contrary. And as our first year in Spain neared an end, I brooded that this was no way for a man to spend his prime, not when he could be in Paris enjoying perfume rather than the stale air of hostage quarters. My muse agreed, for I was unable to wrest a line of poetry from her that first year, perhaps because I spent all my wits reciting too-familiar poetry and retelling stale tales to the two restless boys.

Besides my repertoire there was little occasion for amusement inside our fortress chamber, which had one high window with heavy bars set deep into thick stone, and through which the children could see only if I stood upon a stool and hoisted them on my shoulders one boy at a time.

Once when I lifted Henri until his eyes reached the rim of the window he called down, "Look, there is a glorious sunset tonight. The sky is smoky gold like a topaz but with streaks of purple in it!" His feet were planted firmly on my shoulders, his hands clasped around the rusted iron window-bars to give us both support.

"Alain," he sighed, "I wish you could stand on my back and see outside, but I am too small to hold you."

Only once did the Dauphin mount my shoulders to look from the window. He peered into the courtyard and reported that soon there would be some kind of celebration, for he could see the seats and colored bunting which foretold a tournament.

Suddenly he lost interest in the world outside our cell and cried with fright, "Father told you to take care of me. What if I fall and break my neck?"

"Then I would become the Dauphin," Henri said dryly.

The only diversion permitted to us was attendance at Mass each Sunday, when as the only lay worshipers we were led by guards into a small chapel within the fortress. Once in those four years we were granted confession, though I admit I did not insist. I had not confessed to a priest since assuming my position in court, but in that dreary fortress— as if I'd been given a taste of purgatory before being cast into hell—I found myself craving the blessing of a universal church that enfolds Frenchman and Spaniard alike.

On that single occasion of atonement, at Christmastime of our second year, I gave my confession to the priest in very rusty Latin and afterward wondered at how refreshed my soul felt for its unburdening.

The Dauphin refused to accompany us, claiming that his father and Aunt Marguerite were in sympathy with the Reformers.

"The old church is nearly dead," he said, "and when I am King I shall favor the new."

"What is wrong with the old?" asked Henri. "The past is better than this? What do we have to look forward to? The Mass is the same now and forever, and the incense and bells and glass windows are beautiful old things I can trust."

"How can you even make a proper confession?" the Dauphin sneered. "You only know a little boy's Latin so you won't be able to speak to the priest here. But I've had one more year of Latin than you, so if I wanted to I could give confession, but I don't want to."

"Then you are a worse sinner than I am," Henri said, "I want to but cannot, while you are able but will not."

"My little brother is becoming a hair-splitting papist." The Dauphin yawned. "Pity poor France if I fall and break my neck."

During the time of our captivity while we waited for release, the King concerned himself mainly with his own recovery, which consisted primarily of a dalliance with a new mistress named Anne.

Pope Clement, as expected, absolved the King from the oath he had taken in Madrid. Upon receiving word that the treaty was annulled, Charles raged that François was no gentleman and that according to the agreement he should return to prison, which of course the King was unwilling to do. This resulted in our relocation to quarters even lower in the fortress, a windowless chamber where we slept at night to the sound of scurrying rats.

No longer allowed the courtesy of attending Mass on Sundays, even the Dauphin missed the fragrance of incense and melting beeswax.

Our worsened situation was not Charles's only revenge for the broken treaty. Since that act was sanctioned by the Pope, he sent his army to sack Rome and ordered the imprisonment of Pope Clement. François was bound to defend the Pope in his hour of need, and in acknowledgment of this obligation, the King of France challenged the King of Spain to a duel.

Of course, it was unthinkable for two monarchs to risk their lives in a single combat even though outrage had followed outrage, so another solution had to be found. While the flamboyant King of France pressed on loudly in his contest of words against the King of Spain, the Queen Mother quietly negotiated with Marguerite of Austria, aunt to Charles, and the two women forged an agreement. This new treaty, proposed to both François and Charles in lieu of the shattered Treaty of Madrid, was deemed acceptable by both parties. After four years in Spain we would soon be free.

When that day came, the same river faced us and the same mirror image of a barge appeared across the water, but no one was seated within and the other barge did not stir. Instead, we saw a welcoming crowd of our own countrymen and women, richly dressed, waving as we approached the shore. As we neared the bank it was clear that the King was not among them.

"He would not trouble himself to meet us," Henri said angrily, holding back disappointed tears.

"Would you want the monarch to risk harm?" said the Dauphin as we stepped from the barge and into the welcoming throng. He instinctively stood erect before his father's subjects. Henri appeared disturbed by the confusion and held tightly to my hand, then loosened his grip when he recognized a woman who approached him. Henri stared intently. She was indeed beautiful, though nearer my age than his; in fact, she was almost old enough to be Henri's mother, but in no other way did she resemble the plain Queen Claude, this woman on the shore so graceful and distantly cool named Diane de Poitiers.

Lessons Learned In Exile

THE SEINE SPARKLED in midday sunlight as we crossed a bridge lined precariously with shops. When we passed the Louvre, young Henri was the first to notice the architectural modifications of the building, which had been completed during our absence. I wondered what other changes we might find.

The King received us with great ceremony, and for three days and nights he celebrated with banquets and dancers, musicians, jesters, and clowns. Continuous sporting matches filled the afternoon programs. I was fatigued by the constant activity but assumed the young princes enjoyed themselves, though I knew each one celebrated in a manner befitting his respective nature.

For my part and after months of deprivation, I

watched the elegant noblemen and their beautiful ladies as they bowed and turned to the music in a sumptuous swirl of fabrics. My eyes devoured the hues of the gowns: saffron yellow, indigo blue, Armenian scarlet. Throats shimmered with Egyptian emeralds, clusters of deep red rubies, ropes of luminous pearls. I could hardly contain my joy.

But I noticed Henri's sullen face, and it dawned on me that his only hours of happiness since our return were spent riding along on a hunt, when he was transformed into the congenial boy we remembered from before his mother's death, before the ordeal of imprisonment in Madrid. The Dauphin thrilled to the welcoming pageantry, but young Henri sat stone-faced and grim; it may have been too early to judge, but already some people said that in Spain Henri had become as gloomy as a Spaniard.

Other disturbing thoughts tormented the young prince, for while the rest of us mindlessly followed the entertainers' routines, Henri brooded over the announcement of his betrothal to the niece of Pope Clement. Her name was Catherine, of the Florentine Medici family, and the girl was reported to be short with heavy features and the unattractively protruding Medici eyes.

Thus far Henri's life had granted him few pleasures, and none appeared on the horizon. His brother would inherit the throne while he would always remain the second son and, because of his subdued nature, rarely enjoy his outgoing father's approval.

An exception was their mutual love of the hunt, and from an early age he had taken great interest in the King's architectural projects. Henri was especially fascinated by an old lodge located in the countryside at Fontainebleau, a crumbling ruin that the King had discovered one day while riding. It is said that on that day years ago the King commanded his entire entourage to halt while he dismounted, after which he spent the entire afternoon exploring the abandoned rooms of some long-dead feudal lord. True to his impulsive nature and penchant for ambitious undertakings, the King vowed to transform the ruin into a royal hunting lodge. Fortunately for Henri, a grand hunt was planned at Fontainebleau to crown our homecoming, and in one rare hour of intimacy, Henri and his royal father would ride their horses to a lather, side by side.

As I settled into my new quarters, my old room having been occupied by another man for several years, I was handed a packet of letters that had arrived in my absence. One was from my family, informing me of the birth of my first nephew. The other two were from Michel.

August 1527

My Dear Alain,

Lately I have practiced in Carcassonne on this discouraging sojourn through Languedoc. On any street I travel here I pass a niche, and within each niche sits a statue, for this city has assembled an army of saints to wage battle against the pestilence.

Michel's reputation as healer had spread through the marketplace of provincial gossip, so that upon his arrival in the walled city he was greeted as if dispatched by Saint Adrian himself. But in Carcassonne as in Narbonne his gift for healing was slandered by the local doctors. His initial acceptance by local residents had deluded Michel into thinking that this city might become his safe haven; he was fatigued and needed to gather the strength to continue his work. He decided to stay only a few more days after discovering that both reputation and resentment had followed him, and after determining that Carcassonne provided no access to the teachings he sought. With regret he departed for Toulouse, leaving his patients to their fate in less skilled and less caring hands.

The second letter, dated spring of 1528, seemed more hopeful:

My Dear Alain,

The city of Toulouse might be my final destination in what has seemed an interminable journey, for here I have found a second home. At first I slept in a bare room, for I prefer austerity when traveling, but within the month a local banker provided lodgings in gratitude for my treatment of his wife. When I declined his offer he said, "You were sent by providence. Do not refuse my hospitality." I surmise that he hopes to guarantee the health of his family by having me close at hand.

Michel accepted the offer although wary of comfort and even more suspicious of gifts, which often come tied with an invisible bow of indebtedness. Of course, such indebtedness is the basis of my uncle's life, and now mine. In any case, under such patronage Michel's weakened health was fully restored. He was allotted two rooms for his personal use and the service of an old housekeeper to tend to his needs. Each night after making the round of patients he would return to his quarters, where the old woman had dusted the chairs and chests and smoothed his bed. If the night was cool, a bed warmer would be heating the linens, and a meal and a mug of spiced wine waiting on the reading table beside a trimmed oil lamp.

In such unexpected domestic comfort Michel made great strides in his work. His patron helped him procure copies of rare manuscripts on the subject of herbal medicines, and he resumed the study of the forbidden branches of astrology in the privacy of his room.

Coupled with the daily tasks of examining and treating the sick, this routine of work and reflection expanded Michel's insights into planetary influences, herbs, and man's physical vulnerabilities. He became more receptive to the hidden potency of plants and herbs. He experimented with compounds, and this led him to devise a remarkable treatment for the plague.

THE PATIENT WHO inspired this remedy was a young priest who was saved from oblivion only after Michel's first three attempts resulted in no improvement. Then on his fourth visit, as he swabbed the dark pustules with a recommended ointment of little efficacy, he allowed his thoughts to wander randomly as if seeking relief from the discouragement of the work.

Michel had once told me about the process whereby images come forth and revolve before him, much like turning an astrolabe in your hands, or more like phases of a dream. So it was while attending this patient that in a waking dream he envisioned the legs and arms of the stricken cleric as an abstract shape that transformed into the limbs of a sapling. From this point of departure other vernal images played upon his mind: fragments of memory, a reverie of ferns and blossoms, then Michel heard a phrase as audibly as if a human voice had spoken to him, though no one was present but the unconscious young priest. The voice said, "Rose of Sharon, Damascus Rose." The phrase echoed in his mind, and he knew roses were needed for the cure.

The prescription was simple but locating the ingredients was not. "You seek the unattainable," he was told. "Roses are not to be found around here at this time of year."

Not easily dissuaded, for so certain was he of his mission, Michel found a sympathetic stranger who recommended dried petals preserved for perfume, and the name of a perfumer who might be able to provide them. Soon he stood in a workshop among vials and vats of scent, where the owner was pleased to see a customer after conducting little business in recent months.

From inside a cabinet he brought out a large coffer and removed the lid to reveal a mass of withered petals. No doubt the perfumer thought Michel's request odd, but he agreed to grind the petals into powder and provide them to an apothecary, who would then add specified ingredients and press the powder into lozenges. The lozenges would be dissolved in a patient's mouth.

This became the basis for another night of vigil, for when one lozenge was gone, Michel replaced it with another. By dawn there were signs of improvement, then a time of waiting. Michel would not deem his treatment effective until he saw the man, days later and unaided, walk across the room.

The perfumer, however, did not wait until Michel had pronounced the rose lozenges proven and instead began touting packets containing them as "the famous rose pills of Doctor Nostradamus." The cure by roses became a much-heralded treatment, partly due to this hawking, though local physicians openly derided it and claimed the plague had run its course. Weary of slander, Michel decided to leave Toulouse for Montpellier, where despite his disagreement with so many of the professors, he resolved not to dispute them and accomplish the completion of his medical degree.

My Dear Alain,

My travels have taken me throughout our homeland and to cities in Languedoc that otherwise I would not have seen. I have been rewarded with gold from those who could pay, and rewarded with gratitude when patients could not afford my fee.

Now that I have earned a reputation as a healer, I have decided to return to Montpellier to complete that unfinished task.

Tonight a small incident evoked a memory of St. Rémy. As I dozed before the fire grate, the housekeeper called my name and I woke with a start. She gave me a sweet, served upon a saucer, baked for the occasion of my departure. I bit into the crust and recognized the flavor of a pastry glazed with quince jam.

I regard this as an omen, a cycle of return. Perhaps, my friend, we must revisit our past, the better to understand our tomorrows.

I had barely finished the second letter when a message arrived from my uncle, requiring me to see him at my earliest opportunity. The following day, since the hunting party to Fontainebleau did not require my presence, I borrowed a horse and rode to Léon's home.

The impertinent valet led me into the study, and as

Uncle and I faced each other for the first time in four years I was surprised to see little sign of aging. No doubt he had kept up his rejuvenating program of risky intrigue despite my absence. We embraced, and after he had poured us each a glass of cognac he said, "A libation, to thank the gods for your safe return."

"Finally, you have answered my question about faith." I swirled the amber liquid, cupping my palm around the glass. "You are neither Protestant nor Catholic, you are pagan."

Leon laughed and I joined in, prompting him to note that during the four years away I had not overcome the bad habit of laughing at my own jokes.

"Another toast, then, to our widower-King's new bride, Eleanor," he said, "and the inestimable value of your recent ordeal. Now, tell me about it."

"I have little to recount, for I felt like a blind mole. I saw countryside on the way to and from Madrid, and even then it was dawn or dusk. The only Spaniards I saw were jailers and one priest, and the food, I can tell you, was terrible. They kept us from the mariner's disease by including an occasional handful of kumquats. I have had such an appetite since my return that fear I will soon burst my tunic."

"Perhaps you would prefer to forego tonight's roast lamb and baby onions." He feigned a sniff. "Pity."

"No, I plan on two servings."

He pressed me further for information gleaned during our lost years, specifically about the reactions of the young princes. He had a way of extracting intelligence where there appeared to be none.

"Now that you ask, I did notice different inclinations for it seems our confinement rendered character traits in sharp contrast. I see where you are going with this, so I will leap ahead. When the Dauphin ascends to the throne, he will continue the King's policies intact. But if for some unlikely reason his younger brother should succeed—"

"—you see the likelihood of change." Leon's eyes narrowed into slits.

"Yes," I replied, "for in Spain I learned one thing. Young Henri dotes on the past."

For the next two years I gave little thought to how Henri might alter policy on the off-chance he might inherit the throne. Henri demanded little of me and was rarely on my mind. Meanwhile, the Dauphin required my undivided attention.

In the course of my duties I became an attendant of the Dauphin's wardrobe; I ensured that tailors completed his garments in time for this or that festival or investiture; I saw to it that his hose were tinted to harmonize with each ensemble. Beyond concern for special occasions, I helped manage the everyday business of selection, for the prince changed his appearance, according to his mood, several times each day.

You might conclude that I was a royal lackey with little life of my own, but this is not true. Although the future of my position depended upon current service to the heir apparent, I nonetheless found the time and the means to advance my career and cultivate the affection of two of the many beauties hovering on the outer fringe of the life of the court.

The King was widely known for his dalliances, and this spirit pervaded both the inner and outer circle. Though it may seem that a man like myself had little to offer, nonetheless I was desired—for in this rarified setting, desirability was measured in comeliness and talent for amusement. Though immodest of me to say so, I possessed these qualities to a greater degree than most of my peers. My mastery of the lute and my verses were beginning to be appreciated among the members of the court, and for this reason I became a favorite of one lady-in-waiting. Through her sponsorship I found myself in the courtiers' inner circle. This is how it came about.

One afternoon as I waited by the grass court for the Dauphin to finish his tennis game, I saw a lovely woman glance in my direction and turn my way several times during the game. Afterward she walked toward me.

"They tell me you are Alain Saint-Germain, the young man who cared for the princes in Madrid." She spoke in a voice both confident and modest at the same time.

"I am."

"They tell me that you compose love songs."

"I do."

"Then tell me, are your songs based on truth or are they mere conjecture?"

"To me they are true," I replied, "but a poet's truth is not the same as everyman's."

Someone called her name, but she turned and waved the person away, then directed her green-eyed gaze toward me. "Do you have a song about a courtier's lady in your repertoire? If so, perhaps you would entertain us tomorrow night."

"No, mademoiselle," I began, then intuition made me bold and I added, "for until today, I have not had occasion to love a lady of the court."

She smiled without a blush as though my reply was expected, and I decided this beautiful woman who seemed so fragile with a voice like a small silver bell was actually a cunning creature. Perhaps she would be the one to teach me the advanced lessons in love.

I wondered how to hint at an assignation, but I need not have bothered because she relieved me of the task. As the tennis match closed with the Dauphin a winner, I felt a tug at my sleeve and looked down to see a page who pressed a folded note into my palm then disappeared. The note said she would meet me at sunset. I glanced over to where the Lady Yvette sat across the grassy court. We smiled, and it was agreed.

Lavender and gold clouds of a chilly spring sunset provided soft light at the appointed time, but when I slipped through the unlocked doors and entered the coach house it was already immersed in shadows.

"Here," she called.

My eyes became accustomed to the near darkness as I made my way toward her voice, past shapes crusted in enough gold leaf to dazzle anyone's sight in daylight. Soon I could make out the silhouette of one carriage, and when I reached it found Lady Yvette inside, under a fur robe.

"Why did you choose the coach house?" I asked.

"My cousin supervises the coachmen, and this is dinner time for the men. We have one hour so let us not waste it." She wore only a long cloak, which she slipped off and it soon lay in a heap on the floor.

The hour sped by with both of us lost in pleasure, warming the interior of the coach with lovemaking's scent. By sheer luck the coachmen were late in returning, for we had barely passed through the carriage house door when they turned the corner of the building, laughing and belching. We stood for a few moments in a nearby stand of trees and avoided the rising moonlight.

"Naturally you will come tomorrow," she said, not framed as a question but a command. I responded with a kiss intended to promise another night's fulfillment.

"No, fool, not to slide under my fur," she said with a

dry laugh. "I want you to sing a new song for my friends."

"Naturally," I said, my mind's eye lingering on the remembered impression of our entangled legs.

I waited until a few minutes after she had gone before leaving my hiding place among the trees. *Good fortune continues to find me,* I thought, breathing in the smell of damp bark. My thoughts projected ahead to the next evening. I would be expected to perform in front of an audience of nobles and their haughty retainers, all watching my debut as a poet plunking on the strings of a lute. If they favored me, while I would not be first to make such an ascent from modest beginnings, I would be one of the few.

THE NEXT EVENING, attired in my best tunic and with the beautiful Lady Yvette seated close by, I sang my love song before the men and women of the court. Before beginning, I strummed the lute by way of testing the strings for tone, while I explained that my songs should be regarded as stages in the Platonic ascent of love, wherein a man finds each stage more subtle than the one before, much as the alchemists are said to turn base metal into gold.

I sang of a young man's first love, his awkward discovery of an unknown land.

I sang of the conquests of a university student, who thinks he has fathomed the truth about love.

I sang about falling in love with a married woman, of the dangers and delights.

I sang of the love of a lady of the court, whose grace carries a man to greater heights.

As the last notes from my instrument faded, I heard a woman say in an audible whisper, "You found a treasure." Lady Yvette's friend cast me an inviting smile. My lover reached over and clasped my hand.

"His song is pretty, but he is no philosopher," said a young man who sat with one leg draped over the carved arm of a massive chair. "I say first love must be purer and its motives more sincere, so your analogy breaks down. Therefore first love cannot be compared to the base metal which so-called alchemists turn into gold."

"I agree," said another, "and to attack the analogy further, our poet-who-is-definitely-not-a-philosopher should be informed that he is far from gold when loving a courtier's lady. He has stumbled onto a vein of fool's gold."

The other men joined in the hilarity. Lady Yvette, loyally, did not let go of my hand, but it felt so lifeless that I would rather she had. Stranded in a sea of ridicule, it remained to defend Yvette's honor and mine as well. With a dozen sets of disdainful eyes, and me feeling near to suffocation in my tight velvet tunic, I tried to devise a stance.

Then I recalled the song I had written for Michel. I had almost forgotten it, a poem not written from my own life and memory but from the spring of our friendship and my attempt to grasp his ideals. Though my mouth was dry as a dustball, I managed to speak with a confident air.

"You are right, of course," I said. "Anticipating this argument, and in the spirit of Platonic dialogue, I wish to perform another song to set the analogy straight. The highest form of love leads a man to unite with the Form of his own soul. Even the purity of first love is one step on this divine journey."

After I sang and saw the approval I had aimed for, I rose, took my lute, bowed and left the room. That evening, at least, I played the final note.

The next day I was summoned by the King, a rare occurrence. For some reason I assumed he had been informed of my inconsequential performance the night before, but in any case I felt I had nothing to fear. Nonetheless, I was trembling when I entered his counsel chamber, where he addressed me briefly and bluntly.

"Are you familiar with *The Book of the Courtier,* written by a Florentine called Castiglione?" he asked.

"No, Your Majesty."

"Familiarize yourself with it, for we are told that you show considerable judgment in matters of court life, and have a talent for adapting to changing situations."

I wondered if yesterday's performance had anything to do with my standing on this lush Persian carpet.

"Now we come to the point," he continued. "Our son Henri is not adaptable and lacks appreciation and appetite for the life into which he was born. His brother the

Dauphin has the temperament for conducting himself as royal-born, but Henri withdraws into his books of legends. In light of his forthcoming marriage, we appoint you as his personal *valet de chambre*. Engage him in conversation. Suggest certain intimate activities. Awaken him. Inspire him. Use your proven ingenuity."

"Yes, Your Majesty, I will do my best," I said, feeling overwhelmed by the task ahead.

WHEN I RECEIVED a letter from Michel—I see that it is undated but it must have been in 1529, although lately I lose track of time—he wrote that the students of Montpellier welcomed his return with camaraderie and respect, for his fame during the plague years had preceded him. The professors, however, remembered how intractable he had been the first time around.

In particular, the old doctor (as Michel reminded me) who had once bored me in an anatomy lesson this time greeted him with, "Ah, the famous 'Doctor' Nostradamus. And have the years of plague endowed you with greater wisdom, I pray, than when we saw you last?"

Michel was by then twenty-seven, and several years older than most students in the college of medicine. He resented being regarded as an untried youth by this professor who had remained cloistered within the walls of the college while some of his former students, notably Michel among them, endured hardship and risked their lives to care for victims of the pestilence.

He knew there were many illnesses he had not yet had an occasion to treat, but at the time this seemed to him a minor point. He was still buoyed by his victory in the field, and though tempted to tell the professor that he had succeeded in a far greater test, he decided to humble himself until the examination was complete and he had been awarded the physician's degree and ring.

"I have much to learn," Michel said humbly.

"Then let us see how much you do not know."

THE AUSTERITIES Michel now imposed upon himself to prepare for the remaining examinations would have been impossible four years ago, before he had known the sleepless days and nights when relenting would have meant handing an easy win to Death.

In his small room Michel pored over his books, sleeping only two or three hours a night. To keep himself awake as he studied, he kept small stones or slices of turnip in his mouth. Often he disagreed with the time-worn theories, and now that he had proof to support his own ideas, it required discipline and caution to withhold the controversial answers he longed to give during the examinations; carefully he phrased his replies to fit the examiner's expectations until he possessed the graduate cap and the book of Hippocrates. Finally he was offered a teaching position on the Montpellier faculty; now, Michel believed his voice would be heard.

On the first day standing at the lectern, though Montpellier tradition forbade student discussion in the lecture room, Michel astonished his students by announcing that they were free to formulate critical questions regarding such procedures as the letting of blood and the examination of urine. "If there appears to be another procedure, I will tell you why it will or will not succeed," he said. "If I cannot tell you, I will seek an answer. If I cannot find an answer, I will tell you no one knows."

The wave of murmurs that followed Michel's announcement gave him satisfaction; he would shake these student-physicians from complacence and encourage them to seek truth for themselves rather than accept the threadbare theories of the professors.

He waited. No questions were asked. Even at the insistence of Doctor Nostradamus, the Montpellier students were bound by fear of committing infractions.

Michel was summoned before the dean.

"So, you think your magic tricks will work here," said his superior. "At Montpellier, as are our colleagues in Avignon and Lyons, we are watched closely by agents of the Sorbonne. My dear Doctor Nostradamus, to be a heretic who wears the robe of Hippocrates is no safer than to be one wearing the robes of a Reformer. The latest victims of the Sorbonne are not renegade priests but the readers of the Royal College, men of humanist letters."

"How can this be? The King established the Royal College and made the appointments himself," Michel countered.

"Yes, the King sympathizes with paganism insofar as the artifacts of ancient Greece and Rome are the inspiration for much of his costly architecture, but that is the realm of the eyes, not the soul. The Sorbonne does not want its authority undermined by myths of dead civilizations."

"My views on medicine have nothing to do with religion. I am faithful to the Church."

"Your methods have been likened to witchcraft. Your approach differs both from the proven miracles of our patron saints and also from the Aristotelian system in which we organize our thinking into categories. I've heard that you prescribe some magic talisman given with incantations spoken while waving your hands over the body of a patient."

"Merely a lozenge of rose powder."

"Moreover, you are trying to provoke our students into questioning their superiors. If you value your position at Montpellier, you must abide by our rules."

"I value my position here less than a single dried flower."

"Then I trust you have alternate plans. You are no longer welcome here." His name, he later learned, was scratched from the Montpellier record book.

But just as my fortunes after the years of exile in Spain took a better turn, so did Michel's after his dismissal from Montpellier. In 1532, convinced that some meaning was to be gleaned from the cycle of return to past experiences, he set out for the cities he had visited during the plague years. He was in the prime of his years and relied on the confidence that his reputation would smooth the way. He wrote to me again around this time:

My Dear Alain,

As I travel back through time to Avignon and Carcassonne, to Narbonne and Toulouse, I am glad to be rid of the dank stone buildings and the musty straw of Montpellier's classroom floors. I ride through the countryside as carefree as at any time in my life.

He enjoyed the hearty fare of roadside inns and listened to travelers tales. He journeyed as one of many vagabonds, for the roads of France carried many men who, like himself, had only the vaguest of goals. These were strangers who joined nightly in the wayside inns and recounted tales to each other. He made it his purpose to inquire about medicinal herbs, some with strange and fantastical properties. He collected samples and recorded lore concerning effects and the results of experiments.

Evenings in the crowded inns and peaceful days astride his mule were only a small portion of this time in Michel's life, for along with this retracing of steps he could not avoid confronting illness when his presence became known. Most were common cases and not the deadly disease of earlier years, nor was his work heralded as miraculous, for death kept a distance. Now, when he departed a patient's sickbed, Michel returned to cobbled streets bustling with everyday routine: the sound of vendors, of children, of chore carts. He almost forgot the sight of a death cart's lumbering wheels, the sight of spectral tumbleweeds drifting through desolate streets.

His diligence as a physician earned Michel a modest living and simple satisfactions, the pleasures of peaceful days. He tended few extraordinary ailments and ordinary herbs and remedies usually sufficed. After almost a decade of battle against disease and doctrine as student then itinerant healer and briefly as a professor of medicine, Michel de Nostredame was now a physician quite comfortable with the practice he had shaped for himself.

For three years he lived unchallenged and content. By relinquishing his position at Montpellier, Michel thought he had left behind the sparring of the intellectual arena, but in fact his reputation as a man of independent mind eventually reached the ears of a noted scholar and botanist, who invited Michel first to visit, and then to reside, in the Provençal town of Agen.

November 1533

My Dear Alain,

I have found a town that tempts me to establish residence, as well as a patron under whose guidance my private studies will flourish. His name is César Scaliger."

I knew the name César Scaliger, for he was cited during my student years. His reputation was established by a rebuttal to an essay in which Erasmus had criticized the popular use of Ciceronian Latin. Scaliger claimed that this was the purest language in its most exalted form. He was a man who loved debate.

After Michel had stayed as a guest in Scaliger's home for several weeks, he decided to establish his residency and medical practice. Scaliger proposed a further course of action. He advised Michel to marry and begin a family, and he had a particular young woman in mind.

BEFORE I LEARNED of Michel's betrothal, other nuptials occupied my attention. I took part in preparations for the wedding ceremony of Henri and Catherine de Medici, which took place in Marseilles. Their first meeting began poorly with the two shy young people barely acknowledging each others' presence. Of course, Henri had exhibited little prior interest in young women despite my prompting, while Catherine had other reasons for her shyness. She was the frightened, neglected offspring of a noble family now in decline.

Orphaned at only one month of age when her mother succumbed to syphilis, as had her father mere months before, the child was raised in a convent where she was guarded against those who wished her dead as an end to the Medici line. Clearly such a childhood was not conducive to developing a winsome demeanor, which might have helped Henri emerge from his shell. Catherine was well mannered and well meaning, but quiet and singularly unattractive, two qualities which did not go half the length to win the heart of Henri Duc d' Orleans.

As if to further doom this marriage, when the bridal party returned to Paris, the new Duchess d'Orleans faced a cold reception, for in her entourage she made the mistake of bringing too many Florentines, and this aroused the suspicions of an already mistrusting people. Her fine manners failed to charm the citizens of Paris. They called her "the Florentine" with a sour inflection, little appreciating her superior education and excellent taste.

After her uncle the Pontiff Clement gave the bride in marriage, King François vowed to impose harsher restrictions upon the so-called protestants as a way of honoring this alliance between Rome and France. Until the year before, the King had maintained a policy of tolerance toward the reformers, for he preferred to expend energy in pursuit of pleasure and in the furthering of his architectural projects rather than chase after heretics.

His change of stance on religion caused me concern for, with my duties as attendant to the prince second in line, I wished to attend Michel's forthcoming wedding in Agen and also pay a brief visit to my family in Provence.

Recently it had been reported that Huguenot factions were increasing in that area, and I did not wish to incite the suspicion of eyes watching constantly for lapses that could be construed as heresy. Assured by my uncle that physical proximity to rebellion would not compromise me, I prepared to travel first to Agen.

The journey from Paris to Agen required several days on horseback, and I arrived at the home of Michel de Nostredame just after midday.

He opened the door as I was shaking dust from the brim of my hat. When he saw me, a smile spread slowly across his face, its high cheekbones recalling features I had not seen for several years on a face now etched with a hard-won maturity. We embraced in the doorway and I glanced over his shoulder and past him into the house where three older men and a beautiful young woman sat at a long table.

"You arrive just in time to share our supper," Michel said in a voice more decisive than I remembered. "The servant will bring you a basin," he said, adding with a friendly taunt, "and if you hurry, we'll save you a few bites."

I was shown to a room and the porcelain bowl was soon delivered as promised. I dipped in my hands then splashed cool water onto my face. Quickly I changed into a fresh tunic and cast off my traveling boots in favor of a pair made of soft leather as readily as the infernal hooks and laces would allow.

When I entered the room, Michel led me by the arm to the young woman I came to know as Madeleine, although later some said that was not her baptismal name. As introductions were made, Michel clasped her hand so tightly that her shy smile became pinched with discomfort, though I observed how she tried to hide it.

She was a slender girl clad in a blue-gray dress, with golden hair cascading down her back. As I approached, I saw with surprise that her eyes were of the same serene color as her gown. Here in this distant town, I thought, is a woman worthy of his ideals. She is as beautiful as any pampered woman of the court and, I was certain, more virtuous by far. I could hardly believe that my austere friend had found her in spite of himself. Then I remembered that Scaliger had had a hand in making the match.

I recall most vividly the exchange of tender smiles between Madeleine and Michel; it called to mind a line of the poem I had once written: "when in your eyes I see my gaze, as in a mirror."

Still marveling that this lovely creature would soon marry my friend, I saw Madeleine frown slightly then whisper to Michel, who stooped close to hear. His face flushed and he muttered, "Of course, my dear, forgive me," then released her hand so that she might offer it to me. I found the small hand warmer and more vital than I expected, for at first glance she appeared delicate, her skin so pale and almost translucent that one could see the blood rushing to the skin's surface at the faintest flicker of emotion. Fine veins showed along her temple, and her delicate mouth curved in a gentle smile.

This rush of impressions was cut short as Michel introduced me to the three men in the room: Madeleine's father, her uncle, and César Scaliger. In turn, each of the three men clasped my hand and then returned to some heated discussion that my arrival had interrupted.

I sat beside Michel, who said I would meet Madeleine's mother at some other time. Today she was unable to join us due to an unspecified illness. "The poor woman is of a weak constitution, though I am giving her various remedies to fortify her blood," he said later that evening, causing me to wonder if the delicate Madeleine might someday follow suit.

"Is there no explanation?" I asked.

"She will soon be my mother-in-law," he said under his breath, "so I refrain from calling her malaise a property of her imagination." Later he told me that by refusing to dignify a phantom illness with a false diagnosis he seemed to have seeded her resentment, though he had no idea that for this slight he would pay a high price.

"She tauts me with 'You have saved hundreds from the plague yet you cannot treat one sickly woman?'" He sighed. "Fortunately, Scaliger has endorsed our marriage, and Madeleine's father believes I will make a good husband for his only child."

That same evening after Madeleine and her family had returned to their home, I learned to my surprise that Scaliger was both a man of immense learning and, paradoxically, narrow mind.

"Here is a prime case of impulse to self-display," said Scaliger, who earlier that day had returned from the book fair in Lyons. He sneered as he held up a copy of *Gargantua* by Rabelais, purchased at the fair. It appeared to me that he was outraged by a single fact that had nothing to do with the content of that author's work. Quite simply, no printer in Lyons was interested in publishing César's latest essay.

Confirming my suspicion, he raged, "The printers in Lyons told me the only books that bring profit are romances, inflammatory pamphlets or tales of magic and marvels, while scholarly works do not even pay a printer's costs. The public clamors for this coarse and disgusting verbiage," he said. "Only at the promise of being shocked, aroused or mystified do shoppers spring to open their purses."

I picked up the copy of *Gargantua* and casually leafed through it. I knew Rabelais wrote as an anti-cleric in a time when the Church was under harsh criticism. Rabelais scorned revered institutions, including the rite of marriage, and he poked fun at men like Michel who revered woman as the chaste bride personified by the image of the Virgin. Mocking such a notion, Rabelais reveled in writing tales of cuckoldry.

"His writing offends me," said Michel, who at thirty-one years of age was in thrall to the sacrament he would receive the day after tomorrow. Since our student days in Avignon he had embraced the notion of a woman whose love would inspire his quest for spiritual perfection.

"The man is despicable," Scaliger seethed. "He panders to base minds, appealing to those who desire to read of excreta, debauchery, and sacrilege. Appropriately, he expresses himself in the common language of the street peddler. Since both the content of his writing and its linguistic form are detestable, I see no justification for the publication of his work."

"But many of his sentiments are those of our time," I countered, "as is his choice of the popular form of language, the tongue of living Frenchmen. And while I am faithful to Our Lady, the Church" —I continued with slightly exaggerated piety—"I am also in sympathy with Rabelais's criticism of Church practices. It seems to me that if the Church is to survive, then it must be reformed from within."

Once I had opened my mouth I regretted it. How could I win an argument against this learned man?

Michel seemed to shrink down in his chair while his two friends commenced to lock horns. No doubt he ached to offer an opinion but held back, respecting the conventions of this duel of words, this two-man combat.

"What does a poet know about these matters?" Glaring at me, Scaliger launched into his attack. "Rabelais's work is not a call to reform but a vulgar commercial product. Read his essay on sacred relics and you will see what I mean." Scaliger opened the book to a page he had marked for reference.

I admit that one might call it obscene, peppered as it was with phrases about sacred bones from unspeakable parts of the body, referring to a bit of "sacred shroud" covered with "revered snot," but it was written so cleverly that I could hardly contain my laughter, and when I burst out in guffaws I had to say, "I cannot help but find it amusing."

"Amusing? You are incapable of serious discussion." Turning to Michel he said in a voice quivering with rage, "Your friend the courtier has a facile charm, typical of the breed. With respect for your long-standing friendship I will leave before this discussion devolves further into travesty." He left us alone, silent before the fire dying in the grate.

"For all his brilliance, Scaliger is limited by certain prejudices," Michel remarked when we were alone.

"How can a man of such exalted reputation be so rigid?" I leaned my weary head against the tufted back of the chair.

"When I first met Scaliger I wondered why he had invited me here," he said. "In a manner of speaking, I am an iconoclast myself, but that is in the medical field. He and I agree on other fundamentals."

"Fundamentals?"

Michel sighed. "Agen is a pleasant place, and my opportunities here are unique under the sponsorship of a man who once was physician to the Bishop of Agen. He, too, has formulated certain medicines from herbs, treatments not commonly known."

"That explains a great deal," I said,

"I have resolved my dilemma by keeping many thoughts to myself, and expressing views openly if they fit within the framework of his beliefs. I construct variations of Cesar's point of view."

"Should I pray for the survival of your ideals?"

"Pray for your own, and tell me that you do not live solely for amusement and titillation."

I skirted the issue. "One of my ideals surely must earn your approval, judging by your bride-to-be. We share a love of the beautiful."

"Except you take appearance for beauty," he said and I saw that old judgmental look. "Beauty in a woman inspires a longing for true beauty, the beauty of the soul."

"I am surrounded by beauty. Inspiration is the reason for my constant longing."

"You twist my words," he said irritably.

I apologized and told him that, in fact, I hoped not to lose sight of my ideals, perhaps of a lower order than his but no less authentic. Moreover, I said, I aspired to greater understanding. To make my case, I recalled the day when he stood transfixed and stared at a tangle of watermarks on a stretch of sandy earth. "Years ago I asked about this but you refused to tell me. I want to know what you saw."

He hesitated as if weighing my sincerity. "I saw wavering lines left behind by vanishing rainwater. I knew in dreams I had seen this ancient pattern before. The same pattern is found in traces of rain, in watermarks on all the riverbanks in the world, in the swirls of ocean sand, in the bed of every lake and stream. I knew all the waters of the world in a single instant, and I promised myself never to forget what I saw."

THE MORNING of the ceremony in Agen I woke early in anticipation of a solemn sacrament, one where as a witness I would respectfully bow my head along with other parishioners and spend the day refraining from my repertoire of irreverent rejoinders until I returned to Paris.

I walked the streets of Agen, enjoying the fresh air until finding myself amid the market stalls. There I overheard, as if clinging to me since the previous night, mutterings and ribald talk directed against the Church. It made me wonder where all this rebellious chatter would lead.

Then too, I remembered how a year before this a series of boldly printed placards had appeared on the private door of the King's bedchamber. No one knew how the placards got there, but they denounced the clergy as vile filth, to use a euphemism.

No wonder the King vowed vengeance upon the placardists, not entirely for their sentiments but for penetrating his private quarters. In response to this breach and outrage not only were scores of suspected printers arrested but also for a period of time all printing in France was banned.

A few months later, the King announced his intention to make special amends because the blasphemers remained at large. An expiatory Mass was held in the Cathedral of Notre Dame. The King himself bore glowing tapers in each hand, carrying them as he walked gravely through the center of the grand nave along with his sons, his ambassadors and the nobles of the court. When he reached the altar he turned to the gathered crowd and swore allegiance to the Church, vowing to behead even his own children should they turn into Huguenot sympathizers.

After hearing forbidden phrases muttered in the marketplace of Agen, and recalling the King's vow, I stepped lively and left the rows of produce stalls. It was time to change into appropriate attire.

MICHEL WAS FAR more calm and assured than I would have been in the role of bridegroom. We rode to the cathedral in Scaliger's carriage, and when we arrived Michel stood outside the carved doors and placed his hands on my shoulders.

"I am sparing with shows of emotion," he said, though I knew my presence gave him heart.

After this he continued through the doors and proceeded toward an altar flickering with the glow of candles.

The santuary filled with celebrants honoring Madeleine's family, and in due time the bride and her father appeared. It was an overcast day. Initially the sun could not penetrate the colors embedded in the leaded glass, but finally from overhead a determined shaft of light poured down and split into beams, one tinted rose, another indigo. The colors danced merrily on the couple kneeling below.

Then as suddenly as the light appeared, it vanished behind the clouds.

My stay in Agen was over and my official leave from duties about to end. My friend was now a married man, a groom who adored his bride with such evident joy that he bore little resemblance to the somber Michel I had always known, and I judged the transformation an improvement. But then and now I remain a skeptic. I had known the wings of love to drop the lover back to earth, and I regretted the thought of Michel reverting to his gloomy ways. If he did so then I hoped, for her sake, it would not be soon.

For three years joy and contentment held sway. Madeleine bore two children in good health. Michel's standing in the community grew and his medical practice flourished.

MICHEL LATER CLAIMED that he wrote scores of letters to me during the next decade, though for some reason I received only a half dozen. Perhaps others were written, sent, and lost, for at that time unless you deserved to use a courier for King or Church, your only recourse was to make a small payment to a traveler heading for Paris. In the first of those letters he described his happiness:

My Dear Alain,

After supper each night I watch Madeleine as she sits by the oil lamp near the hearth, working her embroidery. Her needle glints in the firelight as she adds tiny, perfect stitches to the white cloth stretched tight in a wooden hoop on her lap. Soon her handiwork will become a communion dress for our second child.

A page is missing now, but I recall my envy at reading his description of how Madeleine would fold the cloth into a soft bundle; how she would place it upon the chair, touching the back of her hand to her warm forehead, though Michel asked her to sit farther from the hearth. As the hour grew late, she would kiss his cheek then leave Michel alone to study late into the night, or sometimes into the early hours of morning.

In those days Michel walked the streets of Agen as a man beyond reproach. He was highly regarded by the community, and it seemed as if the struggle to defend his reputation lay behind him. But this was not meant to be, and around a year after the second child was born I received a cryptic note:

I write to inform you of the passing of
my beloved wife and children.

I would later learn what his short letter did not disclose.

One morning when Michel awoke and his wife was still asleep he noticed a veil of perspiration on her forehead—lately the weather had been warm—and he instructed the housekeeper to see to the children and let her rest.

He set out to tend to his patients, but two hours later on the other side of town he heard someone call his name. A young colleague stood across the road, his arm raised to catch Michel's attention.

"One of my patients has succumbed, and another is down with a malady that confounds me," he said. "I need your opinion. Please come with me."

Michel hesitated because he had other patients to visit that day, but since these were routine visits the young physician's plea appealed to Michel's sense of duty and, I suspect, it stroked his pride. "Surely this disease will be no stranger to the great Doctor Nostradamus," he told him. "Think of the lives you may save."

Michel reluctantly followed him along a narrow street until they entered a home where an entire family lay prone on rush mats in the close air of sickness.

"The grandmother died yesterday," the young doctor whispered. "The father is worse than when I left him to find you. I watched his wife go through this phase a few hours ago. Her mat is over there," he pointed to a dark corner of the room. "See how red this patient's eyes are, and how his tongue is swollen with a thick coating." The man lay on his back, staring vacantly at the smoke-stained ceiling.

"What is your diagnosis?" the doctor asked. Michel leaned closer and examined the patient, then turned to the adjacent pallet and a young girl whose face glistened, her bedclothes drenched with sweat. "This is the first sign," he said.

Michel remembered the moist sheen on his wife's face that morning. "These symptoms are familiar," he said. His words gave the other doctor false hope.

"Then you know how to treat this."

"I need compounds stored in my herb cabinet," Michel said. "I will return later today."

The young doctor did not try to detain him. Michel hastened from the fetid room and up the street toward his home, where he found Madeleine in bed as he had left her. The housekeeper pressed a wet cloth to her brow.

"She became ill after you left," said the woman "and now her eyes are feverish."

"I have a remedy," Michel said with a feigned confidence intended to calm the housekeeper, who gave him a trusting smile. He took a thin rose lozenge from the box in his cabinet and placed it under Madeleine's tongue.

"Thank Our Lord you know how to cure her, Doctor. The babies seem feverish, too."

Michel had only a few remaining lozenges and knew these were not a proven as a cure for this unknown illness.

Many years ago, he had devised his famous formula in an inspired moment that dawned on him only after many patients had already died. Now the thought uppermost in his mind was that the old grandmother had expired in one short day. He had perhaps that long to devise some remedy. If ever there was a time when he needed composure to meditate on a patient and apply his extensive knowledge of herbal cures then this was the day, but fear rendered him helpless. He entered the quiet storage room to gather his wits and concentrate upon the problem. No answer came.

With little time to spare, Michel administered various treatments to Madeleine in a confusion of compresses and herbal concoctions, with hot bricks to sweat out the illness then cool cloths to reduce the fever. Not once did the housekeeper question Michel's contradictory methods or the different liquids he spooned between his wife's lips, thinking these methods time-tested and true.

Near sunset a pounding on the door interrupted Michel's procedure, and when the housekeeper opened the door the young doctor rushed inside. "Doctor Nostradamus! I waited for you all day—" Then he saw Madeleine. "My God," he swore softly, "this is your wife. The great doctor has no cure."

Michel shook his head. The housekeeper saw this exchange and froze, the cloth she had just removed from Madeleine's forehead hanging limp in her hand. She recoiled in horror, fearing the pestilence.

THE SUN had set hours ago, and in the candlelight shadows danced on Madeleine's pale skin. Steam rose from herbal medications simmering on the hearth, and the cries of the two children tormented Michel nearly to madness. He asked the housekeeper to do one thing then another to assist him, and though she complied he sensed her fear and condemnation.

At last he could bear it no longer. "If you are so concerned for their recovery then go to the church and pray for them, and pray for yourself. Go on, go on, I don't need you here." Silently she drew on her cloak.

Alone with his family in the flickering light and increasingly weak from exhaustion, Michel rested his eyes and despite willing himself to stay awake he briefly dozed. Before he nodded off, he remembered other nights when he first began practicing as a physician. During those early years, the strange sights and sounds of the pestilence had terrified him, but at the same time they held a certain fascination. A decade ago, when he had no home or family of his own, he faced a young man's battle and triumphed.

He remembered the anguished cries and the sight of faces twisted in pain or despair before he devised his rose lozenges, and those who had sacrificed their lives beforehand seemed a cruel but fair exchange for saving the lives of so many later on. But now death stalked his family. His own loved ones would be sacrificed. Even if he could devise a cure it would only occur after failures, and in that time he would lose them. His inner voice was silent as never before.

Just before daybreak, Michel turned back the quilt on Madeleine's bed. Beneath it she remained unconscious. The fever and thrashing were over, and in their passing went the illusion of a struggle for life. By sunrise, Madeleine lay still in his arms.

HE WALKED in the funeral procession behind three biers, two of them so small he was advised to inter them with Madeleine in the same small plot. In his grief he was blind to the accusing stares of his townspeople, unaware that only a few of them defended him by recounting how Doctor Nostradamus had previously saved so many lives. This time the strange illness claimed dozens of victims then ended suddenly, not cured by a remedy but, many said, by providence winning a battle against the angel of darkness.

The end of the pestilence prompted a spate of rumors. Some said the doctor had sacrificed his wife and children to fulfill a pact made with Satan, the price of commanding greater powers bestowed by the dark prince.

Few in Agen had directly known of Michel's healing work during the plague years, though all had heard about his success from others. His more recent reputation was based on providing herbal remedies for common complaints. Still, they had expected him to be infallible—perhaps this was why César Scaliger had invited Michel to Agen—and now he had failed to produce miracles.

The specious rumors persisted, and Michel's adopted home turned ugly before his eyes. Within a few weeks his wife's family had initiated a suit to reclaim her dowry, and even Scaliger turned away from him. Michel's presence was a reminder of César's error in judgment. Despite Scaliger's rejection, Michel remained in Agen, determined not to let falsehoods drive him away.

WEEKS PASSED and no one asked Doctor Nostradamus to attend them with his remedies or attempt any kind of cure. Within a few months, a magistrate ordered Michel to return Madeleine's dowry to her family. He had to sell his home and furnishings to restore the dowry's original value to his in-laws.

After this disheartening litigation, Michel found himself in modest rented lodgings once again and turned to his secret studies as consolation in a period of despair. Then in 1538 he wrote to me again.

My Dear Alain,

Soon I will depart from this place, surrendering another home to my persecutors. Months ago I reached the nadir of suffering and now am finding my way back. At times I wonder if I will emerge a better man.

His departure was not the quiet leave-taking he had

expected when he wrote this letter. The day he planned to depart a minor incident, one that had occurred the previous January, came back to haunt him.

On that previous winter day, Michel had been walking past the workshop of a metal craftsman when he glanced inside and saw finished work strewn about on the floor, a half dozen bronze images of the Virgin surrounded by garbage and rat droppings.

I suspect that Michel was still half deranged by grief over the death of his wife, so at that juncture his personal loss merged with a sense of witnessing an outrage. He barged into the shop, his robe sweeping through scraps of metal and refuse and he confronted the bewildered craftsman, raging at him, "Why do you leave these devotional statues on the floor in filth, as though the Virgin were an unwashed whore?"

"Mind your words, man," cautioned a neighboring shopkeeper who had looked in upon hearing the fracas, and who, restraining Michel, led him away.

In the cool air outside the shop, Michel dimly understood the man's warning words when he said, "The court of the Inquisition has ears behind walls, in the streets, in the most hidden of places."

A few days later a knock on his door brought hopeful alertness coupled with wariness, since Michel rarely had visitors and even more rarely saw a friendly face. When he opened the door, he saw an imposing official clutching a rolled document.

"Michel de Nostredame, called Doctor Nostradamus? I carry a warrant for you to appear before the Court of the Inquisition in Toulouse."

Michel was dumbfounded. "I am under suspicion?"

"Two witnesses have testified against you. I will wait while you make a few arrangements, but only until the sand is the same in both halves." He turned the hourglass over.

Michel wrote a message pleading for help and paid a boy to deliver it to César Scaliger, though Michel expected and received none.

FOR SEVEN DAYS he languished inside a cell in Toulouse, sleeping at night cramped in a miserable position on the cold floor. Finally he was taken from the cell to an ante-room where he waited with a dozen other accused until their names were called and, shaking to the last man, one by one they entered the chamber.

When at last Michel was summoned, he was led toward the bench at the same time as a group of rag-tag young men were being led away; they were tied together at their waists by a connecting length of rope with its free end wrapped around the wrist of a dour old guard.

Michel knelt before the judges with his eyes respectfully cast down. A lengthy detailing of statutes preceded the statement of Michel's alleged crime. While the bailiff droned on, Michel glanced up to see the men who would determine his future. Seated before him at a small, ornate table was the scribe, his head a hairless dome and his mouth framed by parentheses of grim lines. The first joint of his finger marked Michel's case in the thick book of records half-buried beneath his voluminous sleeves.

Above the scribe on a dais draped with velvet sat a high official who dozed in a gilded chair. His snore gave the impression of lax discipline, but compensating for this were four Churchmen in the third tier whose cold expressions conveyed to the accused that they would condemn a man to death without a moment's regret.

Of the three, one looked so intently at Michel that he feared his fate was already sealed. The same official looked away and pored over the papers on his desk, while the bailiff detailed the charge:

"The witness claims that on January 2, 1537, the accused, Michel de Nostredame, cursed the name of the Mother of God. This took place inside the foundry of a smith who works by contract for the Diocese of Agen. The witness has testified that the accused pointed to statues in the process of being repaired and blasphemed the Virgin by using a term for a woman who engages in the lowest profession, the profession of the prostitute, the profession of an unrepentant Mary Magdalene.'"

"How do you plead?" asked the judge in the ornate chair. He had roused himself out of slumber at mention of the lowest profession.

"Those were my words but not my intention, Sir. When I saw the condition of the statues I objected. The smith who testified against me is the blasphemer. He should not touch sacred objects nor have a hand in their repair."

"You are not the witness," said the official as he re-arranged a sheaf of documents. "According to my records, you are the same Michel de Nostredame who resided in Narbonne during the pestilence of 1525. The record also shows that you engaged in unorthodox medical practices in Toulouse during the year 1528."

"Is this true?" asked the official who had shaken Michel's composure with his stare.

"Yes, Your Honor." Michel's voice was barely audible.

"I recommend acquittal," said the same judge who until moments ago had seemed determined to see Michel on the rack. "This man devised an original treatment, a cure that Our Lord granted him the wisdom to formulate. I was one of his many patients in Toulouse during the plague year of 1528, when Doctor Nostradamus saved my life."

AFTER THE COURT of the Inquisition restored Michel's freedom, the prospect of returning to ostracism in Agen seemed scarcely better than the finality of flames. He returned to his room, packed a few belongings, and with a handful of coins hidden in the lining of a riding cloak, he traveled north as if a journey could banish his despair.

Or perhaps the acquittal gave him a renewed sense of

purpose, for once again Michel found himself among the faithful, the adventurers, and other displaced people moving by horse and mule and on foot over country byways.

Thus began a new direction in his quest, and I did not hear from him for another five years. Until then I had no idea of his whereabouts and only that he had departed from Agen. I never doubted that we would see each other at some future time and place.

One night he found himself in the company of three pilgrims and the taller among them asked, "Which shrine is your destination?" to which Michel replied, "I will know the shrine when I see it."

I later learned that his next itinerary began with this chance conversation about pilgrimage. The three devout men were offended by his vague remark and moved their pewter plates to the far end of the communal table. This made room for another sojourner and a conversation that would lead Michel toward the pilgrimage he sought.

"Pardon me, " said a jovial man. "I overheard your clever remark and I must compliment you."

The portly stranger some years older than Michel sat down next to him uninvited. When the innkeeper brought his meal, the man picked up a thick joint of mutton with his hand. "I do not know the underpinnings of your personal philosophy, but possibly you are a hedonist like me," he said, biting off a strip of meat. A glistening stream of juice ran from the corner of his mouth to his chin.

"I am neither pilgrim nor hedonist," Michel replied. "Presently it seems I am beyond the consolation of philosophy, pleasure, or faith."

"No, my good man, pleasure is precisely what one needs in a time of despair, for though you may not know it pleasure begets pleasure and you become happy in spite of yourself."

The stranger's enthusiasm held Michel's interest. "I see you are a man of intelligence," said his new acquaintance. "Someone like you is a rare find for a constant traveler like me. Usually I am surrounded by contentious traders and tedious pilgrims. By the way, what *is* your destination?"

"Truly, I have none."

Michel's answer further delighted him, for he interpreted this state of affairs not as indifference towards the future but, as he himself would intend such a reply, as a willingness to follow any beckoning path.

"I do not wish to pry into your affairs, but if you are continuing north on this road tomorrow then you will pass near a thermal station, a natural spring. I think I will stay at a nearby inn for a week before traveling on to Paris. I have an obligation to my body and must care for it lest ill health limit my pleasure. Perhaps you would care to join me?"

Apparently Michel followed an impulse, much as if I were advising him from afar, for he answered, "I would not mind a few days' respite, though I doubt if your water cure offers relief for my case of despair and regret."

"Nonetheless, you will benefit and at the same time enjoy the delectable food. But let us introduce ourselves. I am Etienne."

Michel gave his full name and saw with relief that Etienne had never heard of him.

They departed early the next morning and by late afternoon had ascended a knoll and saw the thermal station below, its columns of smoke rising from chimneys of several half-timbered buildings. Etienne and Michel led their mules inside a stable located in a compound that had been constructed around the central baths, like walls surrounding a small fortress.

"Which inn do you recommend?" Michel asked. There were several, each with a colorful hanging emblem denoting the name of the inn for the benefit of the unlettered. Among them were the Fleur de Lis, the Black Doe, the Copper Bell and the Blue Halberd.

"I prefer the Black Doe," said Etienne as he gave his mule to a groom, nodding at Michel to do the same. Michel could smell the sulfuric brown water as it gurgled forth from subterranean depths and sent a low-lying veil of steam into the cool afternoon air.

The sun had already dipped behind the brick and timbered inn so the baths were now empty. The stone steps on each end that led into the rectangular pool were wide and shallow, easy to climb for the elderly and infirm that flocked to the baths each year. An uneven border of wooden planks was propped around the hot pool and slanted down to the edge of the water, serving as a simple shelter for a bather who wanted to stand beneath the lean-to as a respite from sun or peering eyes.

They were shown to their rooms, where Michel slept soundly though he woke twice during the night when he smelled the acrid springs and imagined an as-yet-undiscovered treatment, a lost herb, a magical cure. He woke to the sound of bathers entering the water, splashing and carrying on in loud voices. Water lapped repeatedly against the stone walls. Michel glanced from his window and saw that what had appeared as murky brown water the night before seemed clear and sparkling in the sunlight. The pool caught the reflection of a single lime tree.

Soon he was down the stairs, leaving Etienne snoring across the hall. Michel stood at the edge of the pool and saw a steady stream of pure water feeding from a trough by the lime tree into the pool. A dozen ceramic cups were provided for drinking. As he surveyed the thermal baths he forgot Etienne's recommended breakfast of fried bread and instead was drawn to the wooden trough with its outpouring of water, for he knew it flowed from a pure place within the earth. Grasping a cup, submerging it in the trough, he began to administer to his own malady.

He walked past a line of sycamore canes propped against the wall, provided for the aid of elderly bathers, then he found an empty shelter, ducked beneath it, removed his tunic, hose and shoes, set them on a ledge, and sank into the pool. Immersed in warm water, his taut muscles loosened, and within a few minutes his body felt light, his limbs loose and flexible. The water in the cup filled his stomach while the pool bathed his skin. Michel was one of the younger health-seekers. Around him in the swirling waters, making waves or rivulets with their movements, a score of elderly men and a few women were submerged up to their chins.

At midday, Michel retreated from the direct sun and sought the shade of a wooden shelter. Finding one unoccupied, he had just leaned back against the wall and was listening to the sound of water sloshing near his ears when a vendor walked by above.

"Apples," he cried. "Buy my sweet fruit."

Michel peered over his shoulder and saw a basket filled with bright red apples. He was about to buy one when from a nearby shelter a deep voice called, "Take only water the first day. Tomorrow add fruit. Then follow your appetite but in moderation."

"Spoken like a physician," Michel said.

"Not a physician," said the elderly man, "but I have resided here for ten months and have seen as many successful cures. I am one of them. After I arrived I listened, and now I pass that same advice along to you."

"Why did you choose this place?" Michel asked.

"After I became very ill, a friend took me for a consultation with a man named Thières. The man's words were veiled and odd, but I trusted him, and it was by his direction that I came here."

"This wise man told you to come here?"

"Indirectly," he explained. "I remained in the man's home for three days. My host spoke aloud to himself as if I wasn't there, but I paid attention as he ruminated about stars and planets and a mysterious alphabet and a geometrical shapes and their interrelationship with nature. During that time I dreamed unusual dreams, and one morning an answer came from a voice somewhere within me, telling me to seek out the thermal springs."

Michel lay in the warm water, breathing deeply of its vapors. He wondered at how words, whether spoken or written or emanating from some other mysterious source, could alter the course of a person's life. Words snared Michel in the net of the Inquisition and words set him free. Words led this stranger to the sulfur baths and soon would send Michel in the opposite direction over dusty roads to a visionary who might serve as the link between Michel's future and this man's past.

"I am leaving tomorrow," Michel informed Etienne the hedonist that evening as they sat in the Black Doe, Michel holding a mug of the odd-smelling water, Etienne hacking off chunks of the pork stacked on his platter. Etienne responded with the sigh of a man who judged his companion a fool for leaving the thermal station after only one day and without even partaking of a proper meal.

MICHEL'S PILGRIMAGE began the following morning. In the pouch along with his astrolabe he carried a letter of introduction and directions to where the master kept lodgings. He travelled purposefully, and by the time he arrived at Thières's home Michel had regained his concentration and his mind was more lucid than it had been since before his wife's death.

"You are the person I have been expecting," said Thières, directing his assistant to take Michel's cloak and bags. He led his visitor directly down a narrow stone stairway into a subterranean room.

"I sense that you have studied the Mysteries before," Thières said, touching his fingers to his temples, "though I perceive that you have only experienced the Sight from time to time. Tell me of your teachers."

"My grandfather introduced me to the secret studies, but he died when I was a boy. I recall a few fragments of his teachings and the memory of a vision I had as a child. Years later in Toulouse I studied briefly with a teacher of forbidden subjects. I have a limited understanding of so vast a subject, which is why I seek your instruction. I bring an understanding of the prescribing of herbs and the principles of astrology. I learned the first in the field and the second when I was a student in Avignon."

The cellar room with its bookshelf, table, and two chairs was only a few feet across from wall to wall, giving the impression of being inside a grotto. Thières slid the bookshelf forward to disclose a hidden cabinet, from which he removed a deck of cards then spread them in a pattern atop the table. He was silent for a few minutes then began to speak.

"Your token is the cup, which embodies the receptive imagination," said Thières. "Soon events will begin to unfold in your mind's eye like a thousand images on a parchment scroll. You will feel compelled to convey these warnings to others through your writing. You will be praised and vilified. Like Jeremiah, some will dismiss your words while others will try to destroy you."

"Your prediction disturbs me."

"A gift was revealed to you earlier in your life, is this not true?"

"Perhaps so, for when I first became a physician during the pestilence in Narbonne, the first terrible pestilence I had ever witnessed but not the last, I saw hidden relationships between causes and cures. But that was many years ago."

"Your gift remains dormant, awaiting fulfillment of its early promise. Through discipline you will learn to control this vision and the parchment scroll of time will be revealed to you." He pushed the cards aside.

"If this is so then what must I do?"

"I will instruct you in a secret language of signs and shapes and numbers, a mirror of all creation. All living things from a seashell to mankind to a sunflower can be delineated in these terms."

"Would you accept me as your student even if I do not have the means to pay you?" After selling everything he owned to satisfy the demand for principal and interest by his in-laws, Michel had little to his name. "I am poor but resourceful," he added.

"In this work we are obliged to teach qualified pupils who present themselves to us. I cannot shirk this responsibility and retain my power. Whether rich man or poor, your period of study with me will not be of long duration."

Michel wanted to study with Thières until he achieved understanding, not leave with half-answered questions as happened when his grandfather did not live long enough to pass his secrets down to his grandson.

"At this point in your progress you see from a flat surface," Thières said. "I stand on a hill and view the far horizon. In the spread of cards I saw you with other masters, those who will come after me."

"What else do you see on the horizon?"

"Foreknowledge takes many forms. Some events appear as if in a fog. These are tendencies, possibilities. Other events appear in sharp outline, because in the process of formation these potentialities are more solid and represent a greater likelihood. Some are inevitable. "

"You say I will see the future and warn mankind, but I have no desire to do so. Who would invite the curse of

Jeremiah, to foresee the future and be despised or thought a fool?"

"If you refuse my offer, your hunger for answers will increase threefold." His wan smile suggested sympathy. "Michel, your path was determined at birth. Foreknowledge and disseminating this vision is your destiny."

MICHEL REMAINED with Thières for four months. Under this master's guidance, he studied a complex system of correspondences. In one exercise he was instructed to focus his attention upon the inner relationship between colors of the spectrum and the ancient pictorial forms of the Hebrew alphabet.

One night Michel gazed at a candle by his bedside. His meditation that night concerned the letter Tzaddi, the fish and hook, and its correspondence with the color violet.

Hours passed as Michel fought the urge to curl up on his straw bed and sink into a much-needed sleep. Gradually the drowsiness passed and he entered a new realm, the wisdom of midnight beyond dreaming. Suddenly, the white light of the candle shattered into a rainbow arc around the flame. Thières had cautioned Michel not to interrupt his concentration on the gold-white flame for any reason, yet at the moment of this startling manifestation Michel strained his eyes to glimpse the violet band of light lurking at the edge of his vision.

He tried to encompass the outer ring, but the intense

central flame burned into his eyes and pain bore deep into his sockets. Then a veil seemed to fall, and in a trance he sank beneath the flame as though dropping a line into the depths of a molten sea, where many fathoms below he saw Tzaddi as the fish that dwells beneath the surface of consciousness, and as the hook that brings hidden meaning from shadow into light. He had witnessed the perfect order in the heart of chaos.

DURING THE MONTHS of study with Thières, Michel learned of the invisible threads binding all things, animate and inanimate, into a whole. He offered his labor in lieu of payment, but Thieres would not allow him to help with everyday chores. The master explained that unlike the discipline practiced by the Church in its monasteries, the type of thinking Thières was imparting to his student was counter to the logic of everyday thought. It was not based on the linear logic of Aristotle's categories; rather, this discipline led to recognition of what the common world overlooked as dissimilar.

Michel was being trained to cast off everyday assumptions until, unhampered by limitations, his mind would flow from subject to subject and follow the internal language of secret symbols.

But even Thières reminded him, "Eventually, Michel, you must return to the practical world."

Though intrigued by this adventure of the spirit,

eventually Michel became restless and unable to concentrate. When he admitted this to Thières, expecting his teacher to chastise him for lack of dedication, Thieres simply said, "I expected this obstacle. It is time for you to seek your next teacher."

"Then why did you accept me?"

"Because I had a portion of truth to offer but no final answers and, for you, no peace of mind."

MICHEL RETURNED TO THE ROAD again and searched the faces of fellow travelers for a sign. Would this man or that one lead him in the right direction? He sought the company of those who bore a resemblance to his grandfather, to LeCler, to Thières, hoping superficial traits indicated the occult understanding he sought, yet when the sign appeared after weeks of traveling, Michel almost tossed it away.

It was late afternoon on a rainy day near Avignon, where the proximity to the city where he had lived for two years as a student caused Michel to feel that he had traveled in a circle, to feel spent and disillusioned. He sat with a half-dozen other lodgers at an inn, passing the afternoon with mulled wine and conversation as each traveler told a story more exaggerated than the last.

"To be in Venice on a rainy day such as this," began a teller of tales who had not bothered to remove his mud-spattered shoes. The others leaned forward attentively as all caught the whiff of a lewd story in the making.

"When I was in Venice, I would flag down an oarsman and traverse the Grand Canal until I reached the home of the beautiful Raphaella."

"Ah," the men sighed, encouraging the storyteller to spare no detail. He responded to his audience with a no-doubt exaggerated description of the young woman's legs and rump and hips and breasts. "Then, when I arrived at the waterfront entrance to her home to prepare the way for love with an armful of gladioli—" he paused with a frown, prompting one of the rapt listeners to urge, "Tell us quick. What happened next."

"Unfortunately," he shrugged, "when I remember that succulent girl I am repulsed by the thought of her father, the charlatan prophet with his stinking pigeons! He had the gall to claim he could read my miserable future in their droppings or some such nonsense, and he refused to let me court his precious Raphaella."

This allusion to a prophet of Venice intrigued Michel, who wanted to glean more information without rousing the storyteller's jealousy. Mindful of the price of telling a lie, for Thières had told him it would obstruct development of his powers, Michel said, "You certainly tell a rousing tale." As he hoped, this was taken as a compliment.

Michel listened to the increasingly slurred speech of the traveler in the muddy boots for the rest of the evening, though the result was not one shred of useful news. He knew he must find his direction another way, with the hook of understanding. Resolved to do this, the next morning he set out on another quest.

THROUGHOUT THE JOURNEY it seemed that the rain would never cease, nor would Michel's boots ever become dry, yet after a stretch of merciless storms he finally reached the fabled city of Venice. At a distance her domes and spires rose from a pale blue mist. He saw pigeons in every clearing, on ledges, over bridges, in the plaza of San Marco. He walked the narrow alleyways, and while searching for the waterfront entrance to the home of Raffaela and her father he squandered coins on gondoliers who only brought him back to where he had begun.

Somewhere in this labyrinthine city dwelt the man who read the future in the flight of birds. Though he had no information, and though none of the strangers he asked was able to offer a clue, Michel believed that a lost object could be found by another device. With this as his purpose, he found a small room to rent, set out his astrolabe and candle, and began an exercise in concentration to clarify his mind and to focus upon the problem. He repeated the question over and over: "Somewhere in this city is a man who reads the flight of birds. How will I find him?"

In the candle's flame darting images began to appear, images from memory, fragments of conversation, "cages of pigeons" and "a doorway on the Grand Canal." Impressions gleaned on his first day in the city rose and faded in the rainbow arc around the flame: grand and humble buildings, bridges large and small, twisting streets, wide canals, narrow watery passageways.

Michel could hold his eyes open no longer. He extinguished the candle and lay fully clothed atop his bed, hoping to rest a few moments but instead slipping into a deep sleep.

He dreamed of the spires of Venice and of soft rustling wings that grew to a thunderous sound; he saw clouds of birds circling the domes of San Marco a short distance away. They rested on the tops of columns and their sound diminished to a soft rustling once more; the image shrank to a single rooftop with crenellated walls and a small round window overlooking a winding canal. The angle of light indicated midmorning as easterly sunlight rose in the sky behind him. Among the myriad rooftops, behind the wall, stood a man with his young assistant, flushing the pigeons back into their cages.

The following morning Michel woke stiff with chill from an open window. The sun was already rising high in the sky, approaching the angle of light he had seen in his dream. Michel dressed and hurried down the stairs, his destination as clear as if he held written directions.

Walking with the sun at his back toward the Grand Canal, he approached a familiar bridge and was about to cross it but stopped suddenly, uncertain of which course to choose. It seemed his map had been abruptly withdrawn.

He stood still and waited.

Then from above he heard the beating of wings, and over his head a cloud of pigeons rose from a house behind a crenellated wall. He saw his dream in daylight. He reeled with faintness and leaned for support upon a nearby gate. When he felt his strength return, he approached the door of the house and struck its lion-head clapper.

"Signor Giolo is not accepting callers," the servant said curtly.

"Who is it?" Michel heard a woman's musical voice carry to him from inside.

"Tell the lady I am Doctor Nostradamus of Saint-Rémy. Her father is here, for a moment ago I heard pigeons on the roof and they were not enclosed in their cages."

"Venice has thousands of pigeons," said the woman, who emerged from another room and approached Michel in the doorway, no doubt curious about this insistent visitor.

Indeed she was lovely and refined, Michel saw at once, and he knew why the father had rejected the traveler at the roadside inn as a suitor, for that man was unworthy of even touching the edge of her sleeve. As he stood before Raphaella, Michel saw her wary expression soften and thought he had a chance of seeing the master. "I have journeyed far to consult with Signor Giolo."

"In that case I will take you to see him," she said, her appraising look turning to an amused smile.

Once she had led Michel to Giolo's study, however,

the audience began on a discouraging note.

"I am too old to accept another pupil, Doctor Nostradamus." Giolo sighed, as though weary of saying no to so many others who had come before. "I have passed along my secrets to my last apprentice, who has served me for a dozen years." He rubbed his chin as he scrutinized Michel, who asked Signor Giolo to reconsider.

"I sense that your motives are sincere," said Giolo, "not like some who entreat me to teach them because they seek to profit through gambling. But you have traveled far, so I will extend an offer. You may remain as my guest for three days, and during that time you may observe me at work and ask questions."

"I accept your generous offer, Master Giolo," Michel said. He followed the older man to the rooftop, where scores of pigeons were clustered in cages, nibbling at corn and meal, clucking and cooing behind wooden slats. He waited quietly as the master prepared to divine the answer to a petitioner's query. The inquiry concerned the fate of the man's son, who had journeyed to India on a trading expedition six months earlier. During that time there had been no word. Was the young man alive? Was he alive but ill? Was he being held captive?

Giolo's assistant carried a chair onto the roof terrace and placed it in a designated area marked by a painted design. The master seated himself, touched his fingers to his eyelids, and muttered words Michel could not hear. Several minutes passed before Giolo nodded to the assistant, who tossed two handfuls of corn onto the roof then raised the slatted door of a large cage, releasing dozens of the pigeons who swarmed about the corn, puffing up their feathers and bobbing their heads after the bright kernels.

Giolo appeared to be staring at the birds, his eyes glassy, lids partly closed.

Suddenly the scene changed. In a movement the apprentice made without any discernible sign from his master, the young man clapped his hands sharply twice and the pigeons rose from the ground in a startled gray mass.

Giolo lurched forward in his chair and raised his eyes skyward as the flock of pigeons soared upward and scattered across the morning sky. Giolo's lips began to tremble and he spoke inaudibly. The assistant rushed to his side and inscribed notes on a tablet.

After recording Giolo's vision, the man helped his exhausted master rise from the chair then led him down the narrow staircase into the study.

Raphaella told Michel that Giolo must rest now, but he would be willing to discuss the oracle later that afternoon.

MICHEL WAITED impatiently until the servant had removed the remnants of the afternoon meal. "Master Giolo," he said, "may I ask what you saw this morning."

"Amid the frantic confusion of creatures in flight I

saw a young man near death and so far away I knew he would never survive to return home."

Michel remembered the explanation Thières had given him, that some visions are sharp and others obscure. "Did you see this man distinctly?"

"Yes, my vision was clear."

Michel wondered how he knew with such certainty but thought it might seem disrespectful to raise the question, so instead he asked, "How did you learn to read the future in the ascent of birds?"

"When I first set forth as you seek wisdom today, I saw my first master's flock of pigeons and knew this would be my way. I struggled for many long and at times discouraging years to perfect the art of reading their flight."

"You were fortunate to be so single-minded," Michel said. "I seem to have collected nothing but fragments after sitting at the feet of three teachers."

"Some day you may find your voice and your vision, Doctor Nostradamus. Some do and many fail. Perhaps it would benefit your studies to visit a colleague of mine. It is a long journey to Sicily, but you have traveled this far already, and you will find the weather more temperate farther south at this time of year."

"Does he read the flight of birds?"

"No, he reads the message of fire, or what he calls its whisper, the message of smoke. He may be willing to instruct a new acolyte," Giolo said. At dinner he repeated the recommendation that would also serve to send Michel on his way rather than remain longer under the same roof as Giolo's beautiful daughter.

"The Sicilian may be a hermit," he said, "but I urge you to seek him out. Once you are near, any stranger will be able to point the way. I see this destination as your turning point, the one that will lead to your true home."

FOUR DAYS after his arrival in Venice, Michel departed for Calabria, then traveled across the straits of Messina to Adrano at the foot of Mount Etna. Though the distance was great, he eventually found the abode of the hermit, who at once accepted Michel as his student. The man with the red beard who called himself Barra seemed an incarnation of the fiery spirit he summoned from the embers. Despite working in silence, he withheld no secrets and concealed no gestures. Michel observed the man's movements, but wondered if this would in any way help him advance in the occult arts.

Two months passed by uneventfully, then one afternoon Barra motioned for Michel to enter the cluttered chamber he called his sanctum. The last rays of sun were sinking behind the mountain.

Michel sat on the floor in the corner of the room and watched as Barra draped a faded black cape across his shoulders, bringing to mind a penance of ashes. He sprinkled drops of pungent oil into the brass bowl atop a tripod.

Small twigs and bark Barra and Michel had gathered that morning were placed in the brazier, and with a touch of a taper the night's work began. A flame grew like fingers of a hand, spreading from the brass bowl upward as wisps of smoke curled toward the low ceiling.

As his eyes followed the smoke, Michel posed a question: "Will I wander forever, denied understanding?"

From the twigs and smoke came a crackling murmur of sound, a promise. Nostradamus saw a vision of himself in a strange room where he stood beside another tripod, gazing from an upper window that overlooked a thriving town surrounded by lush green fields. The buildings and shops of the town were clear; he had passed this way during his early years of wandering. But if this was the same town he remembered, it was surrounded not by lush greenery but by thirsty, unproductive soil.

Michel knew he had seen his future, and at the same time he knew this was one branch of his path, to see the future of others in a brazier, in the features of the human body, in the alignment of the stars. And now, after countless inns and villages and byways, he also knew the way home. Giolo, had been right; Sicily was his point of return.

ON THE RETURN journey Michel's destiny unfolded before him like the unrolling of a scroll. The third day while traveling back from Adrano on a dusty road, a man approached Michel from the opposite direction.

He traveled alone, and Michel thought this surprising, for both travelers risked injury by journeying without companions on such dangerous roads.

As the man neared, Michel recognized the brown robe of a monastic order. Though he could not see the man's face from such a distance, he knew by his bearing that this was a youth of ambitious nature. Fascinated by the power of the monk's energetic stride, Michel lapsed into a reverie. With the approaching footsteps, the stranger's body dissolved into waves of motion; he melted before Nostradamus's eyes into fluid shapes and colors, from formless gray into purest white, then into crimson as Michel envisioned an older man dressed in papal robes. On his hand, the ring of Saint Peter dazzled Michel's eyes.

"Your Holiness…" Michel knelt at the monk's feet, but the young man did not push Nostradamus aside nor denounce him as a madman. When Michel raised his head and looked into the stranger's eyes, he saw within them an understanding. This man knew his own destiny.

MICHEL TRAVELED ON, driven by his desire to reach the verdant town he had seen in the curling smoke, but before arriving at this destination he would face further challenges.

The sojourn in Italy had spared him from knowledge of a pestilence spread by flooding in a long and sopping springtime, but as he walked once again on French soil a squall assailed him and he sought refuge in a private home surounded by vine-covered walls.

Michel rapped on the heavy door, which soon opened and a tall man filled the doorframe with his blue-robed girth. His extravagant brown beard fit his proportions.

"I am a physician and traveler returning after many months away," Michel said. "I need lodging for the night. Perhaps you could give me directions."

"And at this moment you are wet and cold."

"Yes, and I would appreciate standing near the warmth of your hearth for a while before I travel on. Allow me to introduce myself, I am Michel de Nostredame."

"Your modest request is easily granted, and I insist on providing accomodations. I am honored to meet you, Doctor Nostradamus," said his host, who recognized the traveler by his reputation as a healer.

Michel removed his cloak and sat before the fire, placing his boots as close as practical to dry. Within an hour the rain subsided, and while Michel would have preferred to remain inside by the fire, the squire insisted on a tour around his property, pointing with pride to his livestock.

"I have heard about your effective treatment of patients using herbs, and I also hear that you have predictive powers. Tell me, Doctor Nostradamus, on which of these three piglets will we dine this day?"

A few steps away in the pigsty the squire's two sons were sliding about in the muck, chasing after the three piglets and trying to catch one for the afternoon meal.

"I do not claim to tell the future," Michel said.

"Come, come. Surely magicians tell the future."

Though he had no intention of disputing his host, suddenly he knew the answer. "The black one," Michel said, just as the squire's eldest son held up his catch, a squeaking white pig with brown spots, its legs jerking in desperation as it dangled from the boy's dirty hands.

"Ha! Well, Doctor, your prediction may yet come true —say, next week." The man rubbed his hands together gleefully. "Of course, I asked you which one was to be eaten tonight. Or did I fail to specify?"

"I understood your question, Sir, and my answer remains the same. You will dine this very day on the black pig."

"You are stubborn, Doctor Nostradamus, but don't let this business of predicting come between us, for I am enjoying the diversion of your company," he said, placing his arm around Michel's shoulder as he continued their walk around his property.

Nothing more was said of the piglet until late afternoon when the entire family was seated around the heavily laden table, the children all staring at their distinguished guest. Large dishes brimmed with rustic delicacies. One space remained in the center of the table, reserved for the anticipated arrival of the platter with the spotted roast pig.

The squire poured wine into five shining cups, a hearty red vintage produced on the manor grounds and enjoyed by all but the youngest children.

"Ah, here comes our sweet pig," he announced when the cook appeared with a covered platter and set it down like a centerpiece.

The squire removed the cover of the roast then gasped, dropping the lid into another dish and splashing sauce over the rim. Displayed on the large platter with a crabapple stuffed in its mouth was the roasted black pig.

"Son," growled the host, "where is the white spotted porker, the one you caught this morning?"

"I hit it on the head, Father, and set it on the slab to run its blood, as you taught me how to do."

"But a wolf carried away the pig," said the older boy, "so we had to catch another one."

"Then I suppose I will have to eat my words with a serving of this predestined swine." The squire began to carve. "We have seen an example of your magic, Doctor Nostradamus."

"I am not a magician," Michel said. "I am a physician. You described recent flooding and the return of the pestilence. Tell me where I am needed and tomorrow morning I will depart."

"I am proud to have influenced your decision."

"Save the lives of as many patients as you can," said his wife, "and stop it from reaching us here."

❧

OVERFLOWING RIVERS dispensed the pestilence. Michel traveled through ruined fields, beside rivers swollen with corpses of animals and planks of wood once part of a barn, a shed, or a home. The stench rising from the waters prompted him to gather and inhale the scent of handfuls of pungent wild greens.

The worst of all plague cities was Aix, where the sickness had begun the previous May. By the time of Michel's arrival, the place had become a phantom site of abandoned buildings, its streets wildly grown over with weeds for lack of treading feet. Cobblestones lay about in disrepair, potholes had filled with filth.

So absolute was the despair of the people of Aix that once stricken the victims would abandon all hope of recovery and wrap themselves for death in two winding sheets. This, the most gruesome of plague cities, reeked from its dead, the wild decay, the rank, murky river that continued to feed the pestilence. Michel passed rows of shuttered shops and empty homes; he passed women in tears and bewildered, orphaned children.

When he found that the herbs he pulled from fields and held against his nose helped him breathe along the river road, this encouraged him to try his rose potion again. Uncertain of the cause of its failure in Agen, he decided to modify the formula, and to do so sent a messenger to a town farther away from the river to make arrangements for hundreds of roses, which he had pulverized and mixed with finely ground cypress. To this he added iris of Florence, cloves, and other herbs and shaped the mixture into lozenges. Patients were told to keep a lozenge in the mouth both day and night.

This time the regimen succeeded. Victims of the pestilence began to recover, and patients stopped sewing themseles into winding sheets, waiting to die.

Perhaps his rose formula was truly a miraculous cure, as some claimed. But Michel had known the illusion of performing so-called miracles before facing failure, and so he accepted the gratitude of the town with modesty and conceded that perhaps the plague had run its course by the time he had arrived. Whatever role he might have played, he was gratified to see people reappear and shops gradually reopening. Once again the streets were tamped clean of weeds by the returning bustle of commerce.

MICHEL DICTATED his prescription to the resident doctors, settled his acounts, and continued on to Marseilles. By the time of his arrival there, few patients remained in need of his service.

The maritime city was blessed with cleansing winds from the sea, and in this place Michel made a temporary home to gather his thoughts for a plan conceived on his return journey from Sicily.

He envisioned an almanac, an application of his astral studies to the larger world and its cycles of events. A modest project, and one of limited originality, for such editions written by others were already available, and yet Michel believed that he could bring an uncommon quality to an established form. It would not tax his strength and would allow for expansion. If his spirit were capable of greater vision, it would come to fruition in time.

Waiting for Destiny

IN THOSE YEARS when Michel sought sources of ancient wisdom, I lived for the present and waited for good luck to come my way.

True to my uncle's speculation, Henri Duc d'Orleans suddenly became heir to the throne in the year 1536 when his elder brother, François, died under mysterious circumstances.

Some said the cause was the rapid consumption of iced water following a heated tennis match. Others claimed it was caused by poison in the Dauphin's drinking jar. A man by the name of Monteculi was accused and summarily executed after a confession was wrested from him under torture.

By the time of his ascendancy to Dauphin during his eighteenth year, Henri had been married to Catherine for three years. Consistent with his early habits, he spent as little time with her as possible. He preferred to hunt or play tennis by day; by night, once he had reported to Catherine on the outcome of his day's sport, he would lapse into silence, eat supper with indifference, and retire to his chamber alone.

Occasionally he made nocturnal visits to his wife, but they were so infrequent that the King blamed Henri for Catherine's lack of fecundity. Towards intimacy he showed only distaste, that is until the Lady Diane once again entered his life, the lady who had appeared like a vision of his mother when we first landed after the internment in Spain.

WHEN I FIRST became aware of his friendship with the Lady Diane, I remembered how she had held the eleven-year-old boy in her arms on the banks of the Bidassoa. She was thirty-one then, and married to Louis de Breze, the governor of Normandy. Six years later she was widowed and soon became a frequent visitor to the Valois court.

Unlike the King's mignons, the young and frivolous girls with whom he surrounded himself, Diane was intelligent and mature, not a woman valued for the moment but for her classical grace. She had made a fine art of preserving feminine charm in a world of changing, youthful faces. At thirty-seven she was a handsome woman, and though her hair was prematurely silver, she turned this to advantage by wearing striking costumes of black and white. It was said that she kept her skin radiant and fair by bathing only in milk, and it was said that beneath the layers of fashionable silks her body remained as taut and slim as the ever youthful Huntress, her namesake. With Diane in her role as Diana, eternal nymph, eternal mother, the Dauphin found a solace unattainable with his awkward, coarse-featured bride.

Diane's gravity and wise counsel attracted Henri as did her idealism, her professed fidelity to the Catholic Church and her widow's fidelity to the memory of her husband. She was a symbol of faith and stability to Henri, who thought his father incapable of loyalty or conviction since his sympathy for Catholic or Protestant ways vacillated with each new opportunity to requisition gold from German princes, Parliament or Pope.

The luster of the 1544 treaty of Soissons soon dimmed, and although the King wore the golden collar presented to him by the ruler of Spain for an occasional state dinner, as time passed it became increasingly difficult for him to honor his pledges. There were incidents; the Spanish transgressed. François stayed by the treaty, though Henri regarded his father's resolve as temporary.

"He will break the treaty, for my father cannot keep a promise. His heart is incapable of holding true to course," Henri said to me one day when I accompanied him to Diane's estate at Anet, a few hours away from Paris by coach. The Dauphin went on: "The King writhes in the bondage of vows. Whenever Charles infringes on French soil, as if to convince himself, he says to me: 'When you do a generous thing, my son, you must do it completely and boldly,' but he only subscribes to this until the next Spanish sortie justifies breaking his oath."

Broken promises. Shattered vows. Henri would prefer to live in the age of knights and Crusades, a time (or so he believed) when vows were only broken by death. The Lady Diane was his mistress in the manner of old: a goddess not to be sullied by worldly love. Did she not wear her widow's garb, foreswearing colorful costume? Had she not erected a monument to her husband in Rouen and pledged upon its unveiling that she would honor him by remaining always in mourning?

Ironically, when Diane broke her vow by becoming Henri's lover, Henri was only too ready to accept his lady's rather technical explanation: "I promised only to remain in mourning. I will always wear black."

Overshadowed by his father and at pains to avoid his young wife, Henri established a routine that carried him through the next several years while he waited for the day of his elevation to the throne. The year after the treaty of Soissons, Henri became the last male heir to the French crown when his younger brother, Charles, died during an outbreak of the pestilence.

We who attended the Dauphin during those years were in a constant state of packing his garments for journeys to Diane's chateau. Away from his father's court, Henri became transformed. While we were at Anet, I saw him as an attentive lover and a disciple of the arts. Her estate was a gathering place for poets and philosophers. I yearned to be accepted as a poet and musician among them, though my first duty was attending to Henri's needs.

In Diane's eyes the presence of poet and philosopher was as essential as fine food and statuary, so these things became important to Henri too, although much refinement of phrase and subtlety of theory was lost on him. His favorite book was the romance *Amadis of Gaul,* and his notion of poetry was simple and narrowly framed. Therefore I was surprised when one day as our carriage passed through Rouen upon our return from Anet he said, "Teach me to write poetry."

"You have studied the Latin poets," I began, recalling the classical education upon which his father had insisted, and in which I had drilled him as a boy.

"All I can manage is a weak copy of Cicero or Ovid."

"Then write from your heart," I said. "At first the words will appear stiff and awkward, but as you reach within to find an image to match your sentiments, soon your poem will seem to write itself."

"On the other hand, perhaps I should perfect my Latin," he muttered. "Lady Diane holds scholars in high esteem."

"But French is your tongue," I protested, returning to my usual stance on this subject. "If I may say so, and with all respect, the scholarly role does not suit you as a man who loves the outdoors and the freedom of the hunt."

"In one language or another I must write of my love for her. I pace when we are apart." He turned in the seat for one last glimpse through the gate of her estate before our carriage turned onto the Paris road. We sat in silence a while, with no sound but the droning of cicadas to accompany our twilight ride.

Apparently he had taken to heart my suggestion that he stay true to himself, for he said, "Tomorrow when I will not have a chance to see her I will reread the saga of *Amadis*. Thinking about a lost heroic age brings me closer to my own muse."

I thought of the neglected Catherine who would spend another lonely day and night if Henri carried out his program of solitary reading. As if in anticipation of my objection he said, "The Lady Diane advises me to spend more time with my wife." Apparently she was reminding him that Catherine would be the mother of his sons.

Henri's melancholy vanished during each sojourn to Anet. While François held court in the Louvre, in Fontainebleau, in the chateaux of the Loire amid silken crowds of girls and fawning attendants, Henri held court in Normandy surrounded by myths of another age.

Sculptures cast in the image of Diana and the Stag adorned Lady Diane's garden among chestnut and maple trees. The slender goddess gazed down, gracing the visitor with her chaste and beguiling smile. From paintings on the walls, frescoes on the ceiling, on the sensuously curved vases, the inlaid faces of clocks, and the vast expanse of tapestries, one was almost overwhelmed with images of the goddess in her many guises. Sometimes she was portrayed with a slim, boyish body while other times she was shown as a tender motherly figure with ample breasts, caring for the gentle forest creatures.

Within the grounds and halls of her estate, one could never forget Diana. Her legend filled Henri's eyes when they shared intimate moments within her bedchamber. While the real Diane lay beneath silken coverlets, Henri saw beyond her to the posters of the great bed where four winsome goddesses gazed ardently toward him.

Each day brought a feast of poetry and entertainment, delicacies prepared expressly to Henri's taste. This was a kingdom with no other King or Queen, a place where schedules of court were dismissed except for the program determined by Henri's whim. While life at Anet revolved around him, Diane quietly groomed him to her specifications both as her lover and as eventual King.

❧

THE OLD ORDER neared an end. François ringed himself more closely with beauty, as though the vitality of youth could somehow prevent his death. He lay striken in his grand bed, his face ghastly against a changing mound of snowy pillows.

When sunset approached on what proved to be his last day, I was called to his room where I sat on the far side of the chamber and played my lute softly while the changing parade glided by in elegant gowns, stopping at his bedside for a last farewell.

Later that evening a page was sent for Henri. I overheard the King tell his physicians that he was profoundly weak and must speak to his son at once.

Henri entered the room and made a slight bow, one properly respectful yet distant. The tragedy of the moment did not offset years of resentment, bitter memories of the hostage years in Spain, the favoritism shown to Henri's elder brother, a lifetime of misunderstandings.

"Move close and listen well." François spoke softly and his son did his bidding. "In earlier days when my mind was clear I spoke to you of the craft of kingship. You may have forgotten my words or disregarded them from defiance, but if you remember only two things when I am gone … first, retain my counselors and seek their advice. They are your inheritance. Value them as men who possess great stores of wisdom. You would be discarding a fortune, should you discharge these good men."

Henri, standing uneasily by the side of his father's bed, said nothing in response.

"Second," the King said so faintly that I had to strain to hear. "Learn from my mistakes. If you ignore my words, I promise you nothing but misfortune. My life has been determined by women, by my mother, sister, and many others less enduring but no less formidable. Do not allow this woman to control your life."

"This woman you speak of has the mind of a man," Henri said sharply. "She offers better counsel than the squabbling old men you bequeath to me as royal advisers, and her loyalty to me is absolute. Her wish is only that I might be fulfilled. For herself she seeks no crown. "

The King raised himself with great difficulty from under several layers of quilts.

"She may seek no crown, but her avarice is well known."

"I refuse to listen," Henri said, palm held toward the King like a shield. "Soon I will listen to whomever I choose and similarly bestow my favors. Does it matter if I shower one lady with gifts rather than a hundred as you did? She will cost the treasury less than if I had your playthings to pamper and please."

François collapsed on his pillows and closed his eyes. I tensed with concern but noticed his breathing was even. It seemed he was gathering strength for resolution.

I looked upon the dying father and his defiant son and, though I am not a religious man, I prayed for the grace of reconciliation in these last minutes of a shared lifetime. Into their angry silence I urged the softest possible music from my instrument.

At last the King sighed and said, "By dawn there will be a new regime."

My music filled the empty space until Henri whispered, "The new regime may be less grand than yours, Father, but I must be true to myself. I will consider your advice but I will act as my conscience bids me."

"Finally," said the King, "I cannot ask for more."

PLEASING HENRI lay worlds beyond the many talents of Catherine de Medici. She had perfect manners, a keen mind, meticulous grooming, and with her lavish gowns she even succeeded in disguising her unattractive figure, but she was always somber, and perhaps this was the single key to her failure in Henri's eyes.

I think it was less her plainness that repulsed him than another quality, one reminding him of too much of himself, the motherless and almost fatherless child. In Marseilles when he had first looked into the face of the orphaned girl, pawn of her uncle Pope Clement, he saw no light or hope. They had both known a form of imprisonment and subsequent resignation as children. Henri had turned inward and found solace in a brooding piety and, later, he found consolation in the arms of his mistress, Lady Diane.

As she matured, Catherine would seek out sorcerers and seers for assurance of future happiness: "Will I bear sons?" she asked the astrologers. "Will I be Queen Regent?"

Catherine's first ten years of marriage had been barren, and for this the citizens of Paris cursed the Florentine for bringing bad blood to the French royal family. Rumors had almost convinced Catherine that she was tainted until, discouraged, she sought an audience with her father-in-law King François, shortly before he died.

In that audience she offered to retreat to a convent so that Henri might remarry and provide France with an heir, but when she made this offer and the King refused her request, a curse seemed to lift as if she believed he had faith in her after all. Within a year she bore Henri a daughter. In following years there were two more daughters, then her first son. In fulfilling her role as mother to a future monarch she earned the right to be called Queen Consort, despite another woman who had captured her husband's love.

Gossip and petty stories about Catherine were plentiful in the compound of Anet, where I spent a great deal of time in attendance to the Dauphin; that is, before he gave Diane the lovely Chateau de Chenonceau in the valley of the Loire. Word had it that Lady Diane had a platoon of spies who observed Catherine's daily actions. Her primary purpose in this was to control the education of the royal children. Perhaps one might call this a rather grandmotherly interest, for she was around that age in relation to the royal offspring; or perhaps her interest was due to Diane's self-appointed role as godmother, for it was at her insistence that Henri had entered his wife's bedchamber to produce the royal children. In any case, it became the special concern of Diane de Poitiers to select and manipulate the attendants who provided the royal childrens' education.

Surely the Queen was aware of this; it was rumored that she watched her husband's clandestine lovemaking when on occasion Lady Diane was a houseguest in the palace by peering through a peephole in the ceiling of the lovers' suite. In the face of their public dalliance, though her stoicism was remarkable, this strong facade must have masked a sad, sick heart. Her rival was formidable. Diane offered Henri a temple in which he could worship and find peace, and her favors were administered with the detail of an accomplished priestess. She proffered answers when Henri came to her needing advice; she offered herself when he came needing love. But she demanded much of him, and like the goddess of antiquity, she required devotion.

ON THE DAY of Henri's coronation, he impulsively decreed that Diane was to be crowned at his side. His father's advisers fought against such an outrage of custom and law, but he claimed he was otherwise unable to perform the anointing ceremony. At the last, when the advisers' wills had prevailed, he capitulated but made one final effort.

As I helped him prepare for the ceremony, he turned to me in distress and said, "I must send her a message, that I shall always be her subject and her servant, never her ruler."

"Your Highness, hold still," I interjected, slipping an ermine mantle around his shoulders.

"Give me paper and ink," he said, pushing me aside. "I must send her this message or I cannot accept the crown."

I brought paper and writing material, then watched as his hand flew across the parchment, his lips moving in a whisper until the sheet was filled, his confession spent.

"The page will help me dress," he said. "I need you for the more important duty of finding the Lady Diane."

Taking the sealed letter, I ran swiftly through the door. "I rely on you," he called as I ran from his chamber.

It was a difficult task. The Lady Diane was somewhere in the mob of nobles that filled the Cathedral of Rheims, where the royal party had journeyed for the coronation. Beyond the throng of commoners outside, it seemed that all the nobility of France and half that of Europe were within these walls. If I searched for her by myself then I knew there would be only a slim chance of finding her. I needed a platoon of helpers to conduct the search for me while I remained in one place awaiting their reports.

With the folded letter and its royal seal as my authority, I recruited two score of young boys to go into the crowd, charged with the task of finding a beautiful lady with pale hair dressed in black and white.

At that moment I offered a prayer of gratitude for Lady Diane's hypocritical mourning costume. It was surely by her conspicuous dress and her beauty that one of the boys discovered Diane de Poitiers seated with an attendant and led me back to her through the crowd.

"His Majesty sends this letter and begs you to read it at once," I said, slipping it into her gloved hand. I averted my glance as she gently pulled apart the seal and read it, then she refolded the letter and placed it in the folds of her cape.

"Go to him at once," she said with a warm smile. "Tell him all is well. Nothing will change between us."

THREE DAYS LATER I accompanied the King to Anet. As we rode through the countryside, he tapped his fingers restlessly on the carriage seat.

After we arrived, I played music while they dined on dainty quail prepared with berries in a delicate sauce, served at a small candlelit table in Diane's private chamber. I remained to freshen their wineglasses and tend the fire.

"Nothing will change," said Henri, reaffirming his message as he clasped Diane's hand.

"I only agreed to appease you yesterday," she smiled, "for you will change and you must. You must expand your power until you fill France with your dignity and spirit. You will be a triumphant ruler, my dear. The people will remember your reign for generations."

"Why must I change who I am to accomplish this? Is it not sufficient that I am crowned and anointed?"

"No, for you lack…forgive me…magnificence. Show them grandeur and the people will lay down their lives, but show them you are weak and inconsequential and the country will crumble around you."

"What do you propose then, to create such a legendary reign?" The corners of his eyes crinkled in a playful smile, as if daring her to spin one of her clever strategies.

"Stage a series of triumphal entries, a grand tour of your kingdom. Enter each city like a victorious Roman emperor and those who witness the spectacle will remember and tell their children. Capture the imagination of the people. Win their love, as surely as you have won mine."

"I prefer to celebrate in Paris with jousts and tourneys. Dear one, I am not like a pagan emperor but like a Christian knight, a Crusader."

"But tourneys are of the past, my love, and you are more than a knight. You are the liege. There is no Crusade but there are lands to be regained, lands lost by your father. You need not be pagan to control an empire." Her voice softened. "To revere the art and poetry of antiquity is not a pagan act."

"How can I deny this for I am devoted to you," he said, kissing her hand. "You are my own goddess."

"Then harness this power and your reign will shine with a far greater glory than your father's."

ALTHOUGH IT was dated three months earlier, I received one of Michel's letters in early spring of 1548.

December 17, 1547

My Dear Alain,

May this letter find you in good health, and may you continue to thrive in your chosen life. For my part, I have married again. Anne is a widow. We have established our residence at her home in Salon-de-Provence.

He went on to explain that he had reduced his practice to a few patients. Instead of "tending boils" he was now able to devote himself to other pursuits.

I did not hear from him for another two years, when he wrote to me again with details of his progress. This included the completion of an almanac, the conventional kind with advice as to the phases of the moon, when seed should be sown and crops gathered, also auspicious times for other ventures.

He explained that the almanac had been well received in Provence, though he admitted some embarrassment over its popular success. He regarded the work as a modest effort and one in which he was expected to convey the most pedestrian information. He was more enthusiastic about an expanded almanac, and said he had been experimenting with new modes of expression.

He had returned to the classical languages we had once studied together, though his project sounded to me like a patchwork effort with its mix of Latin and Greek words along with phrases in French. He insisted this technique would distinguish his prognostications from those of other almanacs. On this point he wrote:

> Long ago my grandfather taught me to prefer Plato's truth to Aristotle's neat categories. Common knowledge is like a shadow on the mind's wall; the language of symbols and oblique expression are better suited to higher pursuits. But need I point this out to a poet?

It sounded to me as if he had become a dilettante. He began a translation of Horapollo's treatise on Egyptian hieroglyphics. When this was completed, he concentrated on Latin by translating a detailed description of an Italian wedding feast. *What was he doing*, I wondered?

As I read his letter, I detected a scattering of interests, and this was confirmed a few lines later when he wrote:

> If it can be called a curse in the midst of contentment, then I am cursed by only one thing: distractions.

With free time to edit the notes he had collected on compounds and medications, Michel abandoned the Galen translation midway through to edit his pharmacological notes. Along his journeys, many unusual recipes had found their way into his notebooks, among them restoratives, cosmetics and confitures, including the ingredients for the quince jelly Michel had enjoyed on his last night in Toulouse.

Intent upon proving the worth of such recipes, he began to oversee the making of confitures and sweets in his wife's kitchen and the preparation of restoratives whose formulas he had procured over the past several years. So effective were the latter that his wife, delighted with the cosmetic effects, offered samples to her friends.

To put an end to a phase he considered to have been taken up by "wasteful dilettantism," Michel handed his edited collection of prescriptions, recipes and restoratives to a printer, who suggested that for commercial purposes the title should be called *Treatise on Cosmetics*. The manuscript was so unwieldy that the printer recommended publishing a slim edition first which, if it earned back the cost of production, would precede a second and possibly third volume.

SHORTLY AFTER I received Michel's account of his new life and odd ventures in publishing, I learned that the King had taken Lady Diane's advice, and plans for a grand tour of France were underway.

Costume theatrics have never been my forte, but during the months of preparation I learned about the staging of such a series of events. The cost was astonishing, and what was spent on the hundreds of yards of silks, lace, feathers, and other novelties could have kept the entire populace of Paris well attired for a year. Instead, these costumes were to be worn by the royal family and the hundred or so attendants who would comprise a kind of traveling show. The costumes would transform our King and his itinerant court into a tableau of classical personages, with their appropriately garbed retainers.

Finally all the details were ready. Carriages and conveyances were decorated and packed with basic provisions (fresh meats, produce, cheese, and wine would be secured along the way). I took my place in the third carriage behind the King's own, and considered the problem of keeping my white gladiator's tunic clean for the duration of the three-month journey. This was a problem forgotten in the first triumphal entry when dust from carriage wheels and horses' hooves covered commoner and King alike. We simply shook them out and wore them again in the next town on our progression.

By far the most impressive of the triumphal entries was the one staged in Lyons. Cheering townspeople lined the streets as the King's cavalcade paraded by. At the fore, the monarch rode tall and grand in a suit that simulated Roman armor, and at his side dressed in white, with the barest touches of black, reclined the elegantly gowned Lady Diane.

The line of carts decked with blossoms and banners slowly rolled past, bearing noblemen and court officials dressed in ceremonial attire. Each cart was more dust-laden than the one before, and at the end of the train and scheduled to pass through Lyons's triumphal arch so late in the afternoon that it was nearly dusk rode the Queen, her face barely visible in the fading light.

Since the King's party would remain in Lyons for a week, I was granted a few days to visit my family in Saint-Rémy. I rode out on a swift horse the first night after the triumphal entry and by daybreak I was once again in my childhood home.

My parents were old, my father's hair had turned white, and he walked with the aid of a cane. My mother was in good health and as I remembered her, though the years had etched into permanence the kindly lines around her eyes. My sister was now the mother of two children and it was odd to hear two young strangers calling me "Uncle Alain." My sister chided me gently for the scarcity and brevity of the letters I had sent her over the years.

The reunion though brief was joyous, and when I departed on the second day I knew that I desired to spend my later years not in a cold stone dwelling in Paris but in the sweet-scented, windswept land of Provence.

I had two remaining days of leave from my duties and decided to pay Michel a visit, for from Saint-Rémy it was not a hard ride to Salon-de-Provence. I arrived in town as the moon was rising, and to a lone man hurrying down the street I called out, "Where is the home of Michel de Nostredame?"

After hesitating he replied, "Oh, the husband of the Widow Gemelle," then pointed and said, "Her home is the large one, just up the way." Indeed it was a handsome home and I saw that Michel had married well.

"ALAIN!" HE CRIED, surprised at seeing me, for I had had no time to send a message ahead. Inside the foyer he stood back as if to see me more clearly, then shook his head in disbelief. "After all these years, you have hardly changed."

But I had, of course, and my once-boyish features had softened somewhat in the accumulation of years. For Michel it was just the opposite. At forty-five years of age he was a man of great dignity and authority, strongly built where he had once been overly lean. At his temples and along the perimeter of his beard was a shading of gray that reminded me of an artist's rendering of the wise men of old. Had Michel lived at court like me, he would have extinguished this dignifying characteristic with dye and been dimished by the deception.

"Come, I will introduce you to my wife. She already knows all about you and calls you 'my student friend.' She will ask a thousand questions about Paris."

We entered a richly furnished room, where in a large

upholstered chair sat Madame Nostredame, great with child. He brought me to her. "Anne, we have a visitor. May I present Alain Saint-Germain."

"At last!" she said, offering her hand. I could not help contrasting its warmth to that of poor Madeleine's. We exchanged pleasantries over wine, and after a while she excused herself with "I must get my rest. We had several guests for supper and I am fatigued from the effort. "

I expect that she had ample help, however, for I could see into another room where servants polished silver serving pieces. After Anne was gone Michel explained, "My wife's social sphere encompasses bishop and barrister, jeweler and printer, and minor nobility as well. Almost every night our table is set for a dozen guests. I am urged on by these visitors to recount tales of my 'travels and triumphs.' To my surprise, they praise me as teller of tales."

"It is easy for a man of intelligence to capture an audience with a mixture of imagery and measured phrase, but this is my calling, not yours."

"Three years have vanished with nothing to show for it but an almanac, which any simpleton could compile, and a treatise on cosmetics. Our home is constantly bustling with guests and I am unable to concentrate."

"Surely in this large house you could appropriate a quiet room for your library," I remarked.

"I have been reluctant to suggest it. Anne has long been mistress of her home, and she takes great pride in its furnishings and appointment."

We found comfort in eachother's presence, and as we spoke the intervening years almost compressed into one evening's conversation. He told me of his vagabond years, of the man at the thermal baths who had led him to Thières; of the traveler whose vulgar words offered a clue to finding the master who saw the future in the flight of birds; of how he journeyed from Venice to find the recluse in Sicily, who taught him to read the message of smoke and fire.

Although Michel had warned me of his wife's curiosity about Paris, he too asked questions about the city and secret life of the court. I was surprised when he inquired about palace intrigue and my service to Uncle Léon; in particular, he asked my impression of Louis de Condé, who was leader of the protestant movement, and of François Duc de Guise.

"Why do such matters interest you?" I asked.

"Anne's circle of friends includes the Cardinal, who often dines with us and delights in telling of matters relayed by his network of informers. I have cast horoscopes for him."

"The clergy is second to none for plotting," I observed.

"Even though I have, at times, regarded this prelate as an annoying dinner guest, I admit that in casting the star charts of such a highly placed person I find that more speculations about the future of France are finding their way into my notebooks."

At this point he rose from his chair and paced the floor in rhythmic strides. He continued to hold forth, describing his speculations in detail and not noticing how I was so lulled by his predictable movements that I had begun to doze.

"Forgive me," Michel said when I began to snore. "You are weary, and I have become lost in my preoccupations. I will ask someone to prepare your room."

A while later as I lay in a soft bed, I wondered whether I had dispensed bad advice. Words reached my ears from somewere outside my door, and I heard him tell his wife: "I must forego these diversions and resume my work. I require a quiet room away from the traffic of guests, and away from servants cleaning up after the last entertainment and preparing for the next."

"Do I not please you?"Anne said with a note of bewilderment in her voice.

"Yes, but as important as pleasing me, or my pleasing you, is peace of mind. I need time to concentrate on my writing." A silent spell followed. Michel had, perhaps too bluntly, made his point.

NOTHING FURTHER was said of the matter as we ate our breakfast of porridge and cream. Anne appeared subdued. Michel treated her with special tenderness, and I surmised that he regretted stating his case too plainly.

After the meal and just as Anne excused herself to attend to other household matters, an unexpected visitor appeared at the door with hat in hand.

"I seek your advice, Doctor Nostradamus," said the young man. "I believe you are the only person in Salon capable of understanding my vision."

"What is this 'vision' of yours?" Michel tried to disguise his amusement, for this young man who introduced himself as Adam had a shock of red hair that stood up in a wayward tuft.

"The land of Salon is dry, but on either side of the plain the Rhone and Saône rivers flow like blue borders, depositing their nourishment into the sea. If we divert water from these rivers, Doctor Nostradamus, we will create a pattern of waterways across the plain, and land around Salon will no longer suffer from too little rain."

"Why did you come to me?" asked Michel.

"Because you are respected here. I want to irrigate my father's land and the fields of my neighbors. You have applied unconventional methods in your medical practice, I am told. I come to you in the hope of gaining your support."

Without agreeing, Michel said he would consider endorsing the idea and perhaps underwrite the venture. Adam smiled hopefully and replaced the cap over his unruly hair.

"I know you must leave soon," Michel said to me after Adam had departed. "Let us ride out to the plain, for I would like your opinion on this matter."

We rode beyond the half-timbered buildings of the town into a countryside divided into small fields surrounded by a vast expanse of weeds and coarse brush, where a few meager crops struggled to grow in sun-hardened earth.

"This improbable project interests me," Michel said. "I have often dreamed of a waterway. Sometimes I see it from above, like the warp and woof of fabric. At other times in my dream it appears as dried brown scars on the earth, then the marks turn to inked blue lines on parchment, rippling lines of words extending in all directions."

I saw the distant look in his eyes and recalled last night's discussion, but it occurred to me that here was another worldly distraction, another project tempting him away from concentration on the inner life.

"It seems to me that you can afford to give the young man both money and encouragement if you think there is merit to his plan," I suggested. "But Michel, this is his vision. I beg you to return to the pursuit of your own."

THE SLOW journey back to Paris was delayed by Henri's decision to spend a month at the chateau of Blois. During that time I often brooded upon the fate which had granted Michel two families, even though one had been lost, while I remained alone. When Michel wrote me of the birth of his son César, it occurred to me that I might also have a son or daughter, though I had given little thought to the matter for several years.

The incident that made my parenthood possible was a second assignation with Lady Yvette, the woman with whom I had enjoyed a liaison in the royal coach house when I was newly arrived in Paris and barely more than a boy, the woman responsible for my debut as a poet.

Unexpectedly a few years later the lady approached me with an offer. Because her marriage to a much older nobleman had proven unfruitful and she thought her husband might be at fault, she proposed a secret rendezvous.

Flattered to be chosen as surrogate, I agreed to meet. On two occasions our legs became entwined as before, not in a coach but inside a room in the inn of Saint-Michel. Apparently a third meeting was unnecessary, and afterward I gave little mind to the consequences.

Knowing that Michel had sired a child in his forty-fifth year stirred my loneliness or vanity or a combination thereof. After a few discreet inquiries I found out that the Lady Yvette had a fair-haired son of exactly the right age. As small consolation to myself, and perhaps as a boast to Michel, I wrote him of the child, though once I had placed the letter with a traveler bound for Provence, I regretted my candor. I expected his next letter to be far from congratulatory. To my surprise, many months later he wrote:

My Dear Alain,

I understand the pride of siring a son, and I do not judge you for the circumstances of his conception. You have provided an heir for another man, and you wisely keep such information private.

My own son, who is unmistakably of my own blood and bears his father's gray eyes, was nonetheless baptized with another man's given name. I have named him after César Scaliger, for although Scaliger turned away from me after Madeleine's death, believing the lies about witchcraft that swirled around me, nonetheless he was a man of great learning and I admired him. I wish the same legacy for my boy.

You may recall your advice about establishing a quiet place for my study. After you left, the walls dividing several small chambers were torn aside to create one large room in the house. This room has become my library, study, and retreat, and though Anne occasionally objects, some nights a bare cot affords me greater peace than my dear wife's soft bed.

From the second story, he explained, he could see across the rooftops of Salon and gaze into a night sky where fiery constellations slowly progressed past his study window. He worked by a portable coal brazier, his legs wrapped in a blanket throughout many long nights until the morning star reminded him to close his books and claim needed rest.

Surrounding Michel were the manuscripts guarded with care since his student days in Avignon, and others dating from the earlier years when he had studied at his grandfather's side.

He lined the walls with such treasures, their pages fragile and worn. To these he added more rare books, some ferreted from bookstalls in Lyons, some from teachers with whom he made contact through cautiously phrased correspondence. His library grew. Many nights he read unaware of time until collapsing for a few hours of restless sleep.

Then at long last, after decades of study and discouragement, he encountered his destiny:

One night, from a cupboard behind my cot I removed a porphyry bowl. Years ago I had filled it with wood to evoke the message of smoke, but on this night I filled it with water and set it upon a tripod near a candle by the study window. On the surface I saw a rippling reflection of the room around me, but the images were in reverse: the inverted window, and a brownish blur from the leather books on a nearby shelf.

My eyesight became blurred by the twisted images, and I no longer saw this room but a vortex in liquid. Thus the great work came forth, and from images on water, rephrased as an image of fire, I penned my first quatrains:

Seated at night in my private chamber
Alone, bent over the tripod of brass,

A slender flame arises from solitude
Urging forth that which shall not be professed in vain

Poised in the center of the tripod
With scepter I anoint my foot and hand
In fear I commence to tremble
Heavenly Splendor; the divine wisdom is at my side

But Michel's late hours brought accusations from the citizens of Salon, who believed that anyone ruminating over books until sunrise must be a practitioner of the black arts. Another rumor resurfaced: it was said that in his chamber overlooking the town Michel de Nostredame secretly practiced forbidden Jewish rites.

During daylight hours when he chanced to look down from the study window, he occasionally saw someone watching him from the street below. Or if two men stood together on the street, and if one saw Michel appear at his window, an accusing finger might point upward as if to say, "There he is now, working his devilry in daylight!"

Undeterred, Michel wrote day and night and his notebooks swelled. He completed five sections of a work he now envisioned as ten in its completed form, with each section containing one hundred verses. These would not find favor with King or Church, he knew, but he was convinced that his quatrains should be disseminated to anyone with eyes to see or ears to hear. He was a conduit of warnings to mankind, he believed, of prophecies he must mask in cryptic phrases in order to continue his work undeterred.

After the proven success of his almanacs and household formulas, the printer Bonhomme in Lyons was understandably eager to publish his next work. But it turned out that only four of the five sections would fit into the book's allotted signatures. Reluctantly, Michel agreed to publish the truncated version.

The manuscript was set in type in an abbreviated form, and the first edition of *The Prophecies of Michel de Nostredame* appeared in the booksellers stalls early in the year 1555.

LATE ONE MORNING Anne entered Michel's study with a bowl of water and a towel, only to find him asleep, for he had exhausted himself by reading a treatise on Ptolemaic astronomy throughout the night.

"Bonhomme's agent has arrived," she said, shaking him gently. "He brings good news."

Michel rose and splashed cool water onto his face, rubbing away the lethargy of sleep. With the other hand he reached for his soiled robe.

"Wear this instead." She handed him a fresh garment. The room was musty, the chamber pot not emptied for two days. He had insisted on no interruptions.

"You look pale." Anne opened a window to air out the room. "I worry for your health." Fresh air from the window revived him; it had been days since the last time he descended the stairs.

When Michel reached the downstairs foyer, the printer's agent called out in greeting. "Doctor Nostradamus, *The Prophecies* are a great success! We sold our first printing and I took the liberty of authorizing another print run. When will you complete your next volume?"

Michel hesitated. He had been forewarned in a dream that publication of his work would bring fame and infamy. The first phase was now in motion.

"You may announce a forthcoming volume," Michel said at last. "My notebooks overflow with material, but I need at least three months to edit my notes."

"Then let us amend our first agreement and speak of revenue."

"I will represent my husband in this matter," Anne said. "He must concentrate on his work." The agent sighed, knowing she would draw a hard bargain.

As Michel left the room, he heard the printer mention a figure and Anne reply: "Come, come—surely every printer in Lyon would seize the chance to publish my husband's work."

The name Nostradamus was often mentioned in conversations during the early part of 1556, for in March a comet appeared and gave credence to one of his quatrains:

While the star with the bright tail is seen
Three great princes will verge on war
Peace will be dealt a blow from the heavens
Po and Tiber's floods shall leave a serpent on the shore.

During the next three months, while the comet illuminated the sky, the truce between France and Spain was broken, the Tiber and Arno overflowed and—according to reports—a huge snake-like fish appeared on the banks of the Tiber.

"While the star with the bright tail is seen" became a catch phrase for verity, and *The Prophecies* became the darling of the booksellers. Merchants and soldiers and craftsmen alike showed an appetite for the curious poems that hinted at intrigue, war, catastrophe, and the fate of nations.

The courtiers and nobility in my world argued over the meaning of various quatrains. The book was quoted, analyzed, and interpreted in gatherings among all members of society, mainly those who could read but also many who were illiterate. Nonetheless, many remained who either refused to be swept up in the frenzy of predictions or looked upon the work as the inspiration of Satan.

AROUND THE PEAK of the book's popularity I had another occasion to visit Michel at his home in Salon. Soon after my arrival he suggested a long walk, after which he invited me to join him for refreshment in a wine shop.

Once seated, I raised my hand for service. Gold coins weighed heavily in my belt and I wanted to spend them.

"Show me your prophecy trick," I said.

Michel bristled. "My work is not a trick. I *earned* my entry through the portals of time."

This made me wonder if I could sneak through the portals behind him, for such a diversion would serve me well on a dull afternoon when the royal entourage lacked entertainment. After all, I knew how to pepper my poems with Latin and Greek phrases just as he did, so I began to press him for agreement. Our wine arrived, and he sipped his with a wary expression.

"Are you asking me to teach you the art of prophecy?"

"Yes, that would be convenient."

"Not so simple, my friend," he said. "Would you trade your privileged life for years of wandering? Could you find the patience for making calculations to cast even one astrological chart?"

"You wound me," I said, feigning offense. "As usual you dismiss the effort that preceded my own success." We both knew our opposing natures contributed to the bond between us.

Unconvinced of my sincerity, Michel turned down my request, and as a result I have never known the vision of the oracle. Instead, I have settled for his second-hand stories.

∾

MICHEL TOLD ME that when the future began flooding into his mind, many wondrous and terrible sights came unbidden. He became intoxicated with his visions, hundreds of them. Some men accuse him of commercial intent, and I cannot disprove it, but I do believe that he formed the quatrains into the groups that came to be known as Centuries simply to keep himself from going mad.

Sometimes he saw the future in a vessel filled with water, its surface refracted in candlelight. His visions did not discriminate in their mode of delivery and sometimes appeared in mist or smoke or in dreams.

Many of his forecasts derived from the predictable movement of the seven heavenly bodies, their alignments portending world events; he saw the outcome of battles executed with puzzling weaponry, the misadventures of kings and usurpers and tyrants, the fortunes of great towns and strange cities and nations and peoples to us as yet unknown.

These and more, he claimed, were revealed to him. Even when he saw clearly, which was not always, he tempered the meaning of his visions with symbol and allusion. You might say Michel worked like a spider spinning his orb, segment by segment, until it formed the curious poem cycle reaching one thousand quatrains, and stretching forward twice as many years.

By the time I write this document, it is well known that Michel de Nostredame foretold the death of our King.

But Michel's visions also reveal two great cities burning to ashes. He has seen future rulers struck down and witnessed royal beheadings, some of them queenly.

He foresees a tyrant of short stature who trades the garb of a soldier for an ermine-trimmed robe. He has observed a madman leading an army across the Danube, claiming divine right by the iron cross, a madman who exterminates as many lives as those alive today in five countries combined.

Michel has seen weapons soaring overhead, casting down flames from the sky.

He told me he once awoke from a vivid nightmare. In it he saw the silhouette of a city with impossibly tall structures; he watched two towers exploding in flame, people leaping to their deaths. Then the towers, enveloped in black smoke, crashed to the ground.

WITHIN TWO YEARS, the completed volume appeared. *The Prophecies* now consisted of ten sections of one hundred quatrains under the chapter headings of Centuries.

For a long time I told no one of my relationship with Michel; rather, I told no one except my uncle, for he could be trusted not to reveal our pledge of friendship.

Over the years, Léon had become a rather placid old man. Gone was his once-passionate interest in the maneuverings of the court, as though under Henri's reign he was content to relax his vigil. He had long since withdrawn from society and commerce, but my uncle still loved to parry a point, and it was my duty as his nephew and protégé to provoke an occasional debate.

We sat together in his library one night after a meal of grouse stuffed with oysters, and the groom who had once annoyed me (and who had matured into a faithful retainer) had just filled my cup.

When conversation flagged, I opened *The Prophecies* and turned to a passage I had pondered that afternoon, one I found rather fascinating:

The unhappy nuptial shall be celebrated
With great joy, but with sadness at last
The mother shall despise the daughter, Mary
The Apollo dies, our pity vast.

"I find this verse curious," I said, taking up the game of interpret-the-quatrains, a pass-time indulged in by many of us at court. "Mary, the Scots Queen, is not favored by Queen Catherine, mother of Mary's betrothed. In some sense her fiancé, the Dauphin, may seem like a future 'Apollo,' but if this quatrain foreshadows their unhappy marriage, then it follows that it also predicts his death."

"If you subscribe to that kind of equation," he said, "but it seems to me your Nostradamus likes to bewilder the reader with nouns that are verbs and vice versa, so every quatrain could have several meanings. Consider that 'mary' could also mean 'married man,' and if so your interpretation is wrong."

I granted his point and agreed about the tendency to project an outcome once one has a key word, a noun, in mind. It was as though those four lines fit a lock in my presumption.

Next, I selected two more quatrains and read them to him, and at first he said nothing in response. I thought our discussion had ended for the night, but I was wrong.

"These verses about 'hollow mountains in the New City' and the line about 'men waging war from the belly of a fish' arouse my interest," he began, then drew an odd conclusion. "I wonder if some day a tyrant might interpret the phrases to support his reign, to justify his malevolent purpose."

I dismissed my uncle's speculation as an old man's foolish notion and turned to another quatrain, since events in the distant future seemed to be his preference.

In the year 1999 and seven months
From above shall descend a terrifying King
To restore the great leader d'Angolmois
Fore and after, war shall rage without cease.

"I would not brood over this passage, he said. "I take it to be symbolic, given the similarity to the Number of the Beast in Revelation, an inversion of the number 666."

"Symbolic or not, what kind of terrifying King would descend from the skies?" I pressed my point. "And some say the word 'angolmois' is an anagram for the Mongols. Perhaps the world will undergo a period of Oriental terror."

The Orientals are a fastidious people, notably when it comes to keeping accounts. Perhaps an Oriental reign would represent an interval of order," said Léon with an amused smile. "Speaking of accounts, I am concerned about an overdue payment from a relative of the Prince of Condé."

At first it seemed I had underestimated my uncle's ongoing interest in politics, but he was only worried about a business transaction from the past.

Despite the impressive "comet" verse, some people relished criticizing the quatrains. In my circle, the critics fell into two groups: those who considered Nostradamus a charlatan and those who derided him as an inept poet.

Those who curried Lady Diane's favor largely took the latter position. When the court traveled to the Chateau de Chenonceau, where she was now ensconced, entertainers of various sorts, including sophists and poets, arrived by invitation and remained as long as they stayed in her good graces.

Many young men competed for this honor. The taste of rich food lingered in your memory, and accomodations even for transient performers included touches of luxury. Such competition ensured a varied and changing program.

By this time, in 1556, I had become a semi-permanent member of this troupe, although much of my time was spent in Paris tending to official court duties, for naturally my appearances at Chenonceau coincided with the frequent visits of King Henri.

In the evenings Lady Diane would summon a band of sages and wits groomed for the occasion and prepared to hold forth on several topics. When a dozen men and a few beautiful young women had gathered in the great salon—Diane seemed to harbor no jealousy toward young women, being confident about her own unique qualities—someone would propose a subject. We would debate in a civilized fashion, never forgetting that our peers were unimportant and our true audience consisted of a powerful patroness and a rather narrow-minded King. We threaded our way through pitfalls of language and logic, trying to avoid any connotation that might offend King Henri.

Rarely did the King or his mistress participate in our discussions. I am tempted to call the discussions play acting, for the desired effect was one of diversion. Perhaps my long service, beginning when we traveled to Anet and later at Chenonceau, was because of a role I had assumed as unofficial coordinator of the changing troupe. I had come to know the Lady Diane over the span of many years, and I knew she favored resolution of opinion, though before agreement could be reached she savored argument like a bite of pickle during a rich meal.

I can best illustrate this situation by describing what happened one evening. After an ordinary hour of music and poetry followed by a somewhat dry philosophical discussion of Plotinus (which unfortunately caused the King to nod off), I chose a moment when the last and most tedious speaker was clearing his throat and shifted to a newer, livelier topic:

"About this so-called seer Nostradamus, what do you think of the poetic or prophetic content of his work?"

Voices filled the room as everyone began speaking at once. I had not expected such a passionate response.

"His poetry is abominable," said one, twisting his handsome face into a sneer. "He tortures the rhyme to produce his nefarious omens. I only subjected myself to the first few pages, for by then it appeared obvious that this charlatan was serving me his warmed-over bad dreams."

"These are not prophecies," said another man who produced a copy from his doublet, to my surprise. "The event in this particular verse occurred twenty years ago. I heard the story on my father's knee."

The Blond one will war with the Hawk-nose
By a duel, he shall be forced to flee
The exiles will return to their homeland
And the strong shall command the seas

"Who else could this mean but Charles of Spain and

the Turk who was routed in Tunis twenty years ago? This is no prophecy but merely a retelling of old tales."

At this point a lady spoke up. "You are wrong, for the very title, *The Prophecies*, means these events have not yet come to pass. I say it remains for another fair-haired ruler to fulfill that prediction."

"You speak wisely," said a newcomer named Moreau. "I think this Nostradamus likely speaks the truth. He shows us there is no end to war and no safe quarter for tyrants. He shows us how the mighty will fall." He then proceeded to read this quatrain:

> *The Young Lion shall overcome the Old*
> *By a single duel in a martial field*
> *His eye shall be rent in a Golden Cage*
> *Two wounds from one, the cruel death is sealed*

The room became silent. This thoughtless young man had turned our attention to one of the most provocative of the quatrains, the verses some said predict the future death of our King. Though still in his prime, he was sometimes called by the epithet the Old Lion.

"I submit that the first speaker is closer to truth," I said, trying to defang the quatrain. "I think Nostradamus recalls horrible night visions rather than realities, although it is the latter he claims to foretell. He is skilled at contriving puns and in constructing multi-layered allusions, and when mixed all together this bears a closer resemblance to dreams than to actual events in the tangible world."

Moreau did not grasp that I was doing him a favor and reacted with anger. "Nostradamus writes in the language of the prophet and seer, not the language of chronicle or almanac or tales of the fantastical. His images are obscure because his words are revealed to those who have eyes to see and ears to hear." His eyes blazed with passion. Embarassed, we all looked away.

This dashed any hope of continuing the evening's program, which Moreau had ruined. He would not be invited back. At least I could try to change the topic to another quatrain, leaving Henri, our Old Lion, brooding.

"Here," I began, "in this passage he predicts the rise of Venice and says she will reach the stature of Rome. Do you think this is possible?" All agreed such an ascent was unlikely. "And here," I chattered on, "Nostradamus writes of 'an innovation of the age.' I hear that some people have consulted an astronomer's ephemeris, and based on the conjunction of planets mentioned in the subsequent quatrain, it seems this will occur in 1792. But this date is more than two hundred years from now. Who knows if Nostradamus can see what will happen five years from now, or five hundred?"

"I will not be here to find out," said one of the young men, punctuating his point with a bored yawn.

The Lady Diane was obviously displeased with me

for not managing this unpleasant digression—then I saw Moreau was about to open his mouth again, so I tried to bring it to a close by reducing his argument to absurdity.

"Well then, Moreau," I said, "you admit to belief in this superstitious prattle, subscribed to by those who can neither reason soundly nor create poetry from an authentic source, from the soul."

I caught him off guard with my attack, so certain was Moreau that he had uttered the final word. As he gathered his thoughts, I continued to discredit him:

"Your own poetry strikes me as derivative so I conclude that you do not speak from your soul. Nor are your words guided by reason, for you are as superstitious as a peasant. I must conclude that you have neither a rational nor an intuitive basis for anything you have said tonight. Your ideas are baseless."

I turned to my royal audience. The King's grim expression relaxed and he gave forth a deep laugh. "This man is obviously a fool, as you have made plain, and we do not need to listen to …"

"Moreau," I said, filling in the gap.

"We expect him to be gone by sunrise."

I woke early and made it a point to watch Moreau ride away, a few belongings wrapped in a bundle on his saddle. He must have thought until then that an invitation to Lady Diane's shadow court at Chenonceau meant his path to fortune. In a way his departure saddened me, for I was the one who had contrived his banishment and he was cast out, it seemed to me, for speaking the truth.

As if he could hear my thoughts, he turned around and our eyes met. Then he spurred his mount to a lively gallop and rode out of sight. It was done. The incident with Moreau was sufficient weight for my conscience. I decided that if ever called upon to be an apologist for Michel, I would defend him to my last word.

To be practical, however, in the presence of the King I took every precaution to avoid the subject. But around the same time, another royal personage took great interest in Nostradamus. Long the subject of backbiting and cruelty, the Queen Consort's life must have seemed ill starred. No wonder she sought mystical signs of good fortune and consulted seer after seer in hope that one would disclose a better tomorrow.

When *The Prophecies* was published and word of the work reached Catherine, I happened to be the person most convenient for an errand requiring discretion, and so I was dispatched to a bookseller. It came as no surprise to me, then, when I heard through the Lady Diane's informers that the Queen had already sent a message to Michel de Nostredame summoning him for an audience with her.

If previously I spoke of Diane's informers as though they were distant, I have given the wrong impression. My life was spent equally in the two courts, and on the road between Paris and Anet, then later on between the city and Chenonceau. I had influential friends and informants of my own on both ends of the road.

After so many years in court, I found that Uncle Léon's advice had become part of my fiber, like a language learned when one is young. I had become accomplished in the art of acquiring friends and mutually providing those details that assured advantage.

Did my private life consist mainly of culling secrets and advancing favors? Maybe so, for long ago I had ceased to labor over poems in a naive effort to express my "deepest feelings," and when I no longer gave such feelings their due, it seems they ceased to exist. Only on a rare occasion, such as the departure of Moreau, did I desire a return to my old, more innocent and heart-felt self.

I still had occasional lovers, no longer my own age but now all wonderfully nubile and through them I maintained an illusion of youth. I never had to grovel, being acknowledged as having the ear of the King. Many young and ambitious ladies (as well as handsome, ambitious young men) offered me their companionship. It was an equitable arrangement and I wasted no energy on fidelity or vows.

So with my web-like collection of informers, it was not difficult to find the man in charge of Michel's accommodations for his visit with the Queen. It turned that I had helped this person avoid trouble long ago, so he agreed to provide my friend with comfortable quarters in Paris and also the best of roadside inns along the way. The sojourn was to take place in mid-July, when roads are crowded with warm-weather travelers.

"I have secured rooms for Doctor Nostradamus at the inn of Saint-Michel," he said. I knew first-hand of the inn's charming rooms, once the setting of a memorable liaison, and hoped the name would strike Michel as a good omen.

"You need not worry," said the man. "I will provide for your friend as if he were a prince."

A MONTH LATER I remembered how court favors lose their currency over time.

"I am glad to see you," Michel said dryly, "and if I do not appear overly enthusiastic, it is only because I have been bitten by bedbugs and fleas nearly to madness in the accommodations you arranged for me."

I gasped. "How is that possible? I made special arrangements to ensure the speed and comfort of your journey."

"My sojourn was speedy, when I could find no roadside inn and was forced to continue traveling all night. It was comfortable, the one time I slept in a clean bed during the entire trip, and by then I was ill with chilblains."

His eyes suddenly brightened beneath his furrowed brow. "But I forgot about the discomfort of travel when I arrived in Paris and saw the fortunate name of my inn, and now here you are to greet me," he said warmly, grasping my soft upper arm with his hard, taut hand.

"I can hardly believe you are here, after so many years of my extending invitations and you always declining."

"Until I was summoned by the Queen, whose invitation I could not refuse."

THE AUDIENCE took place two days later, and that same night we met for supper. He began by saying, with a glint in his eye, "The Queen was quite magesterial. My wife asked me to remember what she wore."

"But I have no interest in frocks and am waiting to hear what transpired."

"Of course I will tell you, though I expect court matters reach your ears quickly enough. She inquired after her children, and at her request I had prepared their horoscopes from natal information sent to my room the day before. I was awake all night preparing my calculations."

"What did you see—or rather, what did you tell her?"

"I said, 'Your Majesty, all your sons will be kings'."

"Surely that prediction pleased her, but did you see this transpire?

"In part, yes. I saw that three of the four would be crowned King and I pointed out this beneficent aspect in their horoscopes, but I did not tell her the rest." He lowered his voice. "When I consulted my brazier, I saw the stain of early death upon their faces."

I could not help but remark, "Death seems to be the

theme of your life's work, whether you are physicking or prophesying."

WAITING UNTIL he had finished his meal, in case my next topic upset him, I said, "I have read half of the quatrains in *The Prophecies* and I would like to ask the author a few questions."

"I do not feel like an author as much as a conduit."

"Then in your role as scribe, or whatever you prefer to call your part in the process, you have predicted that the world will be destroyed in two thousand years."

"This prophecy should be of little concern to you."

"You are beginning to sound like your critics, who say we will not be around to know which quatrains will be fulfilled in time and which are simply gibberish. But I am someone who tries to defend you, so I expect a few answers. For example, you allude to a series of anti-Christs that will plague the earth at the end of the twentieth century … *in the year 1999 and seven months, from heaven shall come a terrifying king.* What does this mean?"

"This vision like many others was not clear to me. In some instances I could have set down the precise time and locale of a future event, but not this one. I saw a great upheaval taking place around the end of our current millennium. The power I saw was not a man but a force at work over time. I had no name for this and called it 'king'."

"And what of the passage where you name the city of

London and predict a great fire? Why are you specific in some quatrains, evasive in others?"

"At times I could give the vision no name, while others are veiled for the reasons I just told you. I saw clearly the death of England's great Queen, and the impostor who will be executed by their Parliament, and I saw a great fire in the year 1666, though many times the vision is less specific. I only know by the appearance of men and women that these times are far from France and distant in years."

"What is to happen in 1792, and will it be in this land?"

"Because it will occur in this land, I chose not to name it. A queen and king of France will be forced to flee in the face of an insurrection. Many will die, and many of high station will be beheaded. Around the same time as this desecration, the ruling powers of many lands will change."

"What more have you seen that you chose not to tell?"

"I revealed everything I saw, though I often masked the meaning. The inquisition still has eyes and ears."

Despite longing to ask him about my own future, I sensed that the significance of my life paled before his talk of plagues and fires and famines, of demagogues and insurrections and fallen rulers.

"Tell me," I asked, "apart from her offspring, what about the Queen herself. Did you give her good news?"

"I told the Queen that she would realize greater power in her lifetime. She confided that she has an abiding interest in the secret arts and that while I am here I will be protected under her patronage. She also warned me to be wary lest I fall into the wrong hands."

MICHEL ALSO had an audience with the King, and afterward I had no need to coax him for details. He appeared at my door later that same afternoon.

"The audience was brief," he said, seating himself in one of my two chairs. His face looked drawn, his complexion pale. "The King summoned me at the Queen's insistence, but when I arrived he showed little interest."

"I suspect he feigned indifference."

"Perhaps so, for I detected curiosity."

"What was your advice?"

"I spoke of his sons and their promising future, though this made him frown. Perhaps he thinks the Young Lion will be one of his own offspring."

"Is this what you saw?"

"I saw the King fall at the hand of a younger man, and I glimpsed the moment of the mortal blow. I am told the King is not the type of a man to forego the glory of hunt or battlefield."

Michel's compensation amounted to less than half the money he had spent on lodging and meals. To his chagrin, at the end of his stay the proprietor of the inn of Saint-Michel placed a tariff into his hand, a bill that should have been paid by the clerk who owed me the favor.

Even before this finale our time spent together lost its savor. The risk of prolonging his time in Paris obsessed him; he jumped at the slightest sound even while I tried to engage his attention. Then on the day before he left, I heard from a reliable source that the justice of Paris would soon issue a warrant for his detainment. I reported this to Michel, who departed from the city early the following day.

IN THE EARLY spring of 1558 we anxiously awaited information about the armies of Phillip of Spain, reportedly marching toward Paris.

A rumor circulated about the Spanish king's intention to sack the city in retaliation for Henri's march into Italy. Assembled with a fortune borrowed from Anton Fugger of Augsberg, and with the backing of Queen Mary of England, the combined arms of Spaniards and mercenaries could demolish our army. Led by the Duc de Guise, our forces were still in Italy. King Henri recalled de Guise at once; meanwhile, the city braced for siege.

Within the court some held another view. Unlike his father before him, Phillip hated war. He did not enter battle for love of military encounter but to achieve other ends. On his return from Italy, de Guise laid siege to Calais then marched toward Paris to confront Phillip's army, only to discover upon his arrival that Paris was out of danger. Phillip, weary of the campaign, had returned to Spain.

It remained only to reaffirm the respective strengths

of both rulers, acknowledging that Henri's army had the potential of claiming Italy for France, while recognizing Phillip's forces as the potential captors of Paris. It was a show of strength, a brandishing of troops and weaponry, with the result that a treaty was signed in April of 1559, one in which Henri vowed to remain north of the Alps while Phillip agreed to let Henri keep Lorraine and Calais.

The relinquishing of Calais seemed to me a natural product of the contiguity of Spain and France; Calais had been held by England, Phillip's ally, and England lay distantly across an icy channel.

To the eye of common sense, the soil of France and Spain made one flowing vista, broken only by an imaginary line of demarcation.

Coincidentally, I was reflecting on this land bond when someone gave me the news that in recognition of the treaty, Henri would give his daughter Elizabeth to Phillip in marriage and his sister Marguerite to Emanuel Philibert, the Duke of Savoy.

Plans for the festival were made in a manner distinctively the King's. One evening after I had attended His Majesty with an hour of light music, he asked me if I remembered the celebration of his marriage to Catherine. Before I spoke, I hoped that my answer would be satisfactory, for recently he had chided me for spending too much time with her coterie of poets and entertainers.

"I remember it well," I said in a tone that disclosed

neither fondness nor distaste.

"It was a dreary affair, but this wedding festival for my daughter and sister shall be recounted for generations. Wars are fought on distant fields and treaties are made inside palace walls. For this event, the dignitaries of many lands and the people in the streets will turn out and rejoice in our splendor."

He raised his eyes toward a representation on the gilt ceiling of his chamber and said, "It will be a celebration fit for a hero, befitting of Amadis of Gaul himself."

As you now know, the splendor of the wedding celebration took a tragic turn. Exactly as Michel had foretold, though not on a field of battle, a single cruel blow felled the King in a joust, yet it was a death Henri might have chosen for himself if not so soon. This hardly consoled me in grief, for I had served him since he was a boy.

The power of France now lay in Catherine's hands as Queen Regent, for the Dauphin François was not yet of age. The Queen's favorites would soon rise to higher positions and her real or imagined enemies would be cast out. At this time I knew not on which side of the ledger my name would fall.

Two weeks after the King's death, I was summoned to her bedchamber. There, during the early days of mourning, she held informal audiences.

Kneeling by the bedside, I mumbled respectful condolences. Her protruding eyes looked down on me from the high carved bed. "You may rise," she said. I stood with my hands hanging awkwardly at my sides, nearly faint with anticipation. For years my life had been predictable and I was a stranger to such uncertainty.

"You were a favorite of our husband, and you have served us from time to time," she said in a voice so flat in tonality that her words only heightened my fears. "We understand that you were not among the favorites of the widow de Poitiers. Accordingly, you may remain in our service."

I fell to my knees in a suitable gesture of respect, not to mention one of relief, though I was stung to know that I was not regarded as one of Lady Diane's favorites.

"We will expect more of you than poetry," she said. I anticipated some unpleasant intrigue ahead, so her next words were wholly unexpected:

"You are a friend and confidante of Michel de Nostredame, who in the past has advised me on personal matters as well as matters of state. You will arrange for his sojourns to Paris." She looked at me so directly that out of respect I had to look away. Then she added softly, as if to herself, "This Nostradamus must be my ally."

Buoyed by the prospect of seeing him again, I wrote a letter ensuring his safety and arranged to include it with her next official summons.

My new assistant handed me his reply:

My Dear Alain,

I appreciate your guarantee of protection but you must inform the Queen that my failing health prevents me from travelling to Paris.

As a physician, I know no cure for the pain in my joints and the condition caused by the fluids that increasingly distend my limbs. I am confined to my home, where my days and nights are tormented by crowds massed outside, cursing me as the man who prophesied the King's dying, calling me the scribe of Satan.

Her Majesty offers to protect me, but she is in the capital and people detest me where I reside. Nor do I expect to live long and have begun teaching the Mysteries to my student, de Chavigny, though I know many secrets will go with me to the tomb.

The Queen listened to my paraphrase of his letter, which I sweetened to dilute his harsh words. She accepted his excuse with equanimity, but this did not mean she would relinquish her claim.

"Then we will travel to him," she said sharply. "Where does he reside?"

"In Salon-de-Provence, Your Highness." I was astonished at the idea of an official journey to his home, replete with pomp and attendants and all for a few hours spent, presumably, in Michel's confining study. Soon I learned that the Crown maintained a castle in Provence. The audi-ene would be held there.

"We are devising a grand tour to introduce our son to his people. Speak to our secretary and make sure our itinerary includes time for an audience with Michel de Nostredame."

BUT FIVE YEARS elapsed before we actually made the royal progression. The tour was delayed because the sickly François died less than two years after his father, making a widow of his young bride, Mary of the Scots. This brought his brother next in line of succession. He was proclaimed Charles IX and the tour scheduled for the following year.

I found myself with double duty, helping with the details of planning the progression, and also involved in the somber task of disposing of my Uncle Léon's estate. My parents had died a few years before, but somehow their loss affected me less deeply than the death of my uncle, who had advised me, and I him, until his final days.

When I was informed of his considerable debts, I reflected that my information over the years might have led him to grant loans to the wrong clients. Now as his heir I would pay for such misdirection. After selling his lodgings and furnishings to settle his accounts, however, I was still left with a fair sum.

Moreover, I was suddenly faced with my own mortality upon the passing of the last relative of my parents' generation. This was on my mind when I wrote to inform

Michel of the forthcoming royal progression, of my small inheritance, and my desire to return home to Provence.

In his reply he suggested that I purchase a small property near his own. With this in mind, I arranged to secure the parcel he recommended and resolved unfinished business in the city that had served as my second home.

I would leave Paris, however, regretting that my son would never know me. The Lady Yvette was among the few people who acknowledged my departure. In exchange for erasing her beauty, time had made her heart grow kind.

THE ROYAL COMPANY assembled, and we began our journey. Salon-de-Provence was my destination, but until we reached it, I would serve the Queen Regent one last time. This was not my first progression, for I had accompanied Henri to Rouen, Tours, and Lyons many years before, when Diane rode beneath the emblem of the crescent moon and Catherine followed at the rear of the entourage.

But now Lady Diane had been deposed. The jewels Henri had bestowed on her were reclaimed, the Chateau de Chenonceau was in Catherine's hands, and the Queen Regent commanded the front position in the progression, triumphant in widowhood.

For astrological reassurance concerning the future of her children, we turned from the main road toward Salon. I left the entourage at the crossroads. With no difficulty I located Michel's home again. I struck the clapper on his door and waited; soon a young man appeared at the doorway. This must be César, I thought. He resembled his father when Michel was the dark, slim boy who had walked with me in the fields of Saint-Rémy.

"Come in, come in!" I heard an irritated voice call from across the room. I stepped inside to see Michel lying on a cot by the fire, bundled in blankets. He was buried in wool except for his swollen face and hands. I must have looked at him aghast.

"I did not realize you were so ill," I stammered, not knowing whether to embrace him.

"Come close, Alain, do not be offended by my gruffness. To some of us it comes with age."

"But we were born the same year," I protested.

"…with age, pain, and the aggravation of a family." He smiled wanly and his still-alert eyes looked with affection upon the young people, his most tender glance lingering on his daughter. He introduced us then said to them, "Now leave us for a time. The conversation of two old men requires a peaceful setting."

Soon I became accustomed to his occasional grimace of pain and we talked until late in the night. He told me of his fears, not of releasing his hold on life but of relinquishing his place at the head of his family.

"I have become a wealthy man," he said, though in the next breath he expressed worry lest his daughter not be provided a proper dowry, and he went into great detail about the provisions of his will. It occurred to me that the dowry and lawsuit involved in his first marriage might have left a scar. I wondeed if he was confusing them.

"My daughter will never know the truth of the Mysteries, for she is a woman and would be condemned as a witch, but I can give my daughter these treasures to secure her future." He opened a small wooden box with a velvet lining. "I have set aside these gems for her—all but this one." He showed me a violet stone. "The amethyst was the gem favored by the Egyptians for escorting the souls of the dead, and it will accompany me to my grave."

"Do you foresee the time of your death?" I asked.

"I have noted the date on my ephemeris."

I wanted to speak of our former days, but he wanted to talk about death, and perhaps if I knew my own days were numbered then I might think along those lines too.

"What arrangements have you made for your other children," I asked.

"They have been provided for. I will leave César my ring and astrolabe, though he is not of a serious nature."

He had first accused me of this when I was about César's age, and he had never changed his mind.

"All the volumes in my library will be sealed away until my sons reach maturity," he said, "then Anne will decide who will inherit them."

"About the dire events you predicted in *The Prophecies,* is there no hope of averting them? If not then what is the value of prophecy or the purpose of will?"

"I pray many of my predictions will not come to pass."

"Tell me again—as I am unclear—why do some visions of the future become manifest and others do not?"

"The Book of Corinthians tells us 'we know in part and we prophesy in part'," he said. "I have been granted a vision of events that may take place if the pattern of destiny remains unaltered. My vision is one of direction, not destination. Do you remember the green snake we tossed into the air long ago in Saint-Rémy? We expected it to reach the ground but it landed in a tree."

Anne tapped on the door to remind us of the hour.

"Help me to my study before you go," he said.

At the top of the stairway we embraced, and I closed the door behind him.

The next day a coach transported Michel to the crown's southern stronghold, Chateau Lamperie. There he gave another reading of the horoscopes of the Queen Regent and her children.

We had one year to enjoy the wafting scent of lavender fields and share recollections of the years we spent apart. I began a new phase of my journal entries, setting aside the pages I had filled with my adventures in Paris and instead making notes based on what Michel told me. I told him I had kept most of his letters and he was visibly touched.

In July of 1566 he collapsed for the final time while

working at his desk, on which sat an ephemeris with that same day marked with a cross, or so I was told.

Michel's student, de Chavigny, helped the widow arrange Michel's papers, but when he asked for his master's library, the provisions of the will forbade it. The content of the will was as Michel had told me, with one curious amendment: if Anne should bear his posthumous child, it included a formula for reapportioning his estate.

There was no posthumous child. It occurred to me that he could see the fate of kings and world events for hundreds of years, but twice he had been blind to the future of his own family.

We know in part and we prophesy in part.

Assuming my health lasts, I expect to live a few more years. No arcane wisdom assures me of this, for I am not a man given to visions. I have no date marked on my calendar.

I have often thought of Michel de Nostredame and me as the obverse and reverse sides of a coin. His was a defiant face before the world, famous and infamous in his own time. Mine was a face hidden behind great men and women. Michel was a prophet who wrote in a poet's quatrains, and I was an unknown poet who captured small joys and sorrows.

If I had his vision and could see the future, would I find a change of position on the coin? Would my poetry live on and the name of Nostradamus be forgotten?

Nearly three decades ago I wrote a novel based on the life of the sixteenth century seer Michel de Nostredame, known to the world as Nostradamus.

The book was originally published in 1983, when no one could imagine the magnitude of a future act of terrorism that would falsely become associated with his name.

On September 11, 2001, two airliners crashed into the World Trade Center in New York. Within hours, the name of Nostradamus was invoked repeatedly on the Internet, sparking tens of thousands of hits within two days.

It was said that two of his predictions, expressed in cryptic poems or quatrains, foretold the tragedy of the twin towers:

In the first year of the new century and nine months
From the sky will come a great King of Terror
The sky will burn at forty-five degrees
Fire approaches the great new city

In the city of York there will be great collapse
Two twin brothers torn apart by chaos
While the fortress falls, the great leader will succumb
The third big war will begin when the big city is burning

But this pair of quatrains, hailed as the dark prophecy of September 11, turned out to be a hoax. Lines were lifted from unrelated sections of the predictions. The so-called prophecies attributed to him were fakes, shuffled and dealt as a trick hand. Arguably, a thin line separates a hoax from a misinterpretation of the quatrains, but this was a case of intentional deception.

Ever since *The Prophecies* was first introduced in 1555, the quatrains have been interpreted, reinterpreted, and mis-interpreted by people seeking a match between phrases and events, looking for confirmation of the hand of destiny at work in the decisive moments of history.

Almost five hundred years after his birth, the name Nostradamus still resonates. Some say he left behind a roll call of the world's evil rulers and pandemics, its bloody wars and epic disasters. Some call any similarity between predictions and events a mere coincidence.

During the almost thirty years since writing this book I have remained both skeptic and believer. In the Author's Note of the 1983 edition I posed a question: are the predictions of Michel de Nostredame authentic or fraudulent?

I leave it to you to decide, perhaps after you have read the story of a boy who became the man behind the myth.

Allene Symons
March 2011

BIBLIOGRAPHY

Bishop, Morris. *Ronsard: Prince of Poets.* London: Oxford University Press, 1940.

Boman, Throleif. *Hebrew Thought Compared with Greek.* Library of History and Doctrine. Philadelphia: Westminster Press, 1954-1960.

Cheetham, Erika (ed. and trans.) *The Prophecies of Nostradamus.* London. Neville Spearman, Ltd., 1973.

Chomarat, Michel. *Nostradamus Entre Rhone et Saône.* Lyons: Ger Editeur, 1971.

Crouzet, Francois. *Nostradamus Poet Francais.* Paris: Julliard, 1973.

Febvre, Lucien. *Life in Renaissance France.* (ed. and trans. by Marion Rothstein. Cambridge: Harvard University Press, 1977.

Leoni, Edgar. *Nostradamus: Life and Literature.* Smithtown, N.Y.: Exposition Press, 1961.

LeVert, Liberte E. *The Prophecies and Engimas of Nostradamus.* Glen Rock, N.J. Firebell Books, 1979.

Roberts, Henry C. (ed. , interp. and trans.). *The Complete Prophecies of Nostradamus.* Great Neck, N.Y.: Nostradamus, Inc.. 1973.

Strong, Roy C. *Splendor at Court.* Boston: Houghton Mifflin Co., 1973.

Wiley, W.L. *The Gentlemen of Renaissance France.* Cambridge: Harvard University Press, 1954.

www.ingramcontent.com/pod-product-compliance
Lightning Source LLC
Chambersburg PA
CBHW032024120726
47898CB00002BB/661